Olympic Dream

MATT CHRISTOPHER

Illustrated by Karen Meyer

LITTLE, BROWN AND COMPANY

Boston   New York   Toronto   London

To Dominic and Barbara

Text copyright © 1996 by Matthew F. Christopher
Illustrations copyright © 1996 by Karen Meyer

First Edition

Library of Congress Cataloging-in-Publication Data

Christopher, Matt.
    Olympic dream / by Matt Christopher ; illustrated by Karen Meyer. — 1st ed.
        p.   cm.
    Summary: When overweight fourteen-year-old video whiz Doug Cannon is introduced to the sport of cycling he begins a transformation that leads him to health and self-respect.
    ISBN 0-316-14048-1 (hc.) ISBN 0-316-14163-1 (pbk.)
    [1. Bicycles and bicycling — Fiction.   2. Bicycle racing — Fiction.   3. Weight control — Fiction.]   I. Meyer, Karen.
    ill.   II. Title.
PZ7. C45801   1996
[Fic] — dc20   95-45653

10 9 8 7 6 5 4 3 2 1

MV-NY

Published simultaneously in Canada by Little, Brown & Company
(Canada) Limited

Printed in the United States of America

Olympic
Dream

The air rushed by Doug Cannon's face. It felt like a million tiny needles going deeper and deeper into his skin. Each and every downstroke on the pedals strained his whole body. There was no slipstream to encase him in empty air space, to just carry him along. He was out in front of the pack. He set the pace as the race wound to its finish.

There was no looking back. Even though he was in the lead, he couldn't be sure what was taking place behind him. He simply had to press on. With every bit of energy he had left, he had to race for the finish.

But as the road stretched out in front of him in an unbroken ribbon of black, Doug couldn't help drifting back. He was a long, long way from all that had happened to put him where he was — racing as hard and as fast as he could toward the grand finale of all

1

his efforts, the gold medal. Imagine, Doug Cannon, crowning his cycling career with a gold medal in the 2000 International Olympics!

Whoever would have imagined it just a few years ago?

1

Zap!

Score 22,000 and climbing.

Zap! Zap! Zap!

One more purple target and I'll reach the big two-five.

Fourteen-year-old Doug Cannon leaned in toward the video monitor as far as he could. But because of the bulge around his middle, that wasn't as close as he'd like. It was at times like this that he wished he weighed a little less.

There was a lot at stake. Right now he was the top video jock in his class. No one could approach him when it came to high scores. These were the numbers that mattered to him — not the ones on the scales. He clutched the joystick so fiercely he could almost feel it dissolve.

3

But the thought of his oversize midsection had destroyed his focus for a crucial moment.

Blurrrp! GAME OVER.

Rats! In the midst of a supersonic air war, an ordinary widebody had come into the picture from the bottom. It had thrown him for a loop.

Widebody! That's what some of the kids at school called him behind his back. He didn't like it, but what could he do about it? He couldn't fight with half the kids in school, could he?

He never missed those bottom ones. Too bad he couldn't get a little closer. Maybe he ought to change his strategy. Or try a different game.

"Yo, Doug," came a voice from the front of the video arcade. "We're going over to the beach. You coming with us?"

It was Pepper Meade. Pepper was the unspoken leader of the guys in Doug's class at school. They all played most sports together, hung out together. On Monday most of them would be going off to summer hockey camp together — but not Doug. He played goalie on the hockey squad, but only because the school made everyone play on some team. Because of his weight, he wasn't much good at sports. And ex-

4

cept for video games, he didn't think of himself as a competitive person. Still, he was always good-natured and willing to fill a spot on the team. The guys liked him. Most of the time, Doug liked them, too. So when they made wise-guy comments about his size, he swallowed his hurt feelings. No, instead he played along and was always welcome to join in on whatever they were up to.

Pepper was always the ringleader when the guys did get on Doug's case. He was the one who gave him the nickname "Lardy" when they were just little kids. The name had been forgotten by the others over the years, but Doug remembered.

"Go ahead," Doug called back. "I'm just going to play one more game. Maybe I'll catch up."

The school year had just ended at noon. He had the whole summer to hang out at the lake. Right now he was on a hot streak at this video game. He was determined to set a new personal record. It was something he was really good at. This is where he could really shine. Besides, the last thing he wanted to do was walk around in a bathing suit in front of those guys. They would only get on his case, call him "Willie the Whale," and tease him to do a belly

5

flop. So what if he was a lot bigger than most of them?

He reached into his pocket and found it was empty. He'd used up all his money already. Now there was nothing else to do except join the guys at the beach — or go home.

Doug glanced at the machine, sighed, and walked out of the arcade. He shrugged his shoulders and turned in the direction of his house.

The minute he crossed the threshold, he could tell that something was different. Suitcases! There were suitcases, bags, boxes, and a big laundry sack, plus a tennis racket dumped just inside the door. Kate was home!

His sister Kate had just finished her first year of graduate school. She had graduated from State College a year ago and now she was going for her master's degree. Doug knew she was due home that week, but it was still a surprise when he saw her drinking a tall glass of iced tea in the kitchen. Even though there was nine years between them, she treated him like a pal as much as a brother. And she never made wisecracks about his size.

6

There was a strong bond between the two Cannon kids.

"Hey, buddy-boy, how are you doing?" she called over to him. She got up from her chair and opened her arms wide. Their hug was instant and powerful.

"Great," he replied, flopping down on a chair opposite her. As he watched her sip her tea, he noticed a flashing sparkle on her left hand. "Hey, that's a ring," he said, pointing.

She wiggled the third finger of her left hand at him. He could see a thin, gold band with a single diamond smack in the middle.

"Uh-huh," she said with a big smile. "Guess what — I'm engaged."

"Like . . . like . . . you're getting married?"

"You've got it," she said. "The wedding's going to be right here in the backyard, last weekend in August."

"Holy cow!" he shouted. "I'm going to be a — a what? A brother-in-law! Hey, who's the lucky guy?"

"Terry, of course," she said. "You ninny, who'd you think it would be?"

"Just checking," said Doug with a mischievous

7

grin. "Had to make sure you didn't dump him for someone I didn't like. Terry's a great guy. I remember when you first started dating him. You wanted us to get to know each other better, so you sent him over to the arcade one time to give me a lift home. He played a few games before we left. Great hands."

"They'd better be, since he's going to be a doctor," she said.

"I just can't get over it," said Doug. He got up and took the cookie jar off the counter. Dipping in, he took out a couple of oatmeal-raisin cookies. "My big sister getting married!"

"And my little brother is going to be an usher," said Kate.

"What!"

"Yup, Terry's friend Red Roberts is going to be the best man and we want you to be an usher. They're coming for dinner tonight, so you'll get to meet Red. He's going to be a doctor, too, like Terry, and — oh, there's so much to do. Listen, help me drag my stuff upstairs and I'll tell you all about it."

"Sure," said Doug, licking the last cookie crumbs from the corners of his mouth.

As he headed for the doorway, a million thoughts

rushed into Doug's head. School's out. The guys are going off to hockey camp for the summer. Kate's going to get married at the end of August. I'm going to be an usher, like the guy who showed me to my seat at Cousin Hallie's wedding in the big church in town. But Kate's wedding was going to be in the backyard. Maybe I won't have to get all decked out in one of those tuxedos like the ushers in Hallie's wedding. They didn't look all that comfortable. Yeah, and what about standing around for those pictures? Hallie's husband's cousin Timmy looked like a blimp when they lined up for the pictures. They put two little flower girls in front of him and you could still see Timmy on each side of them. Is that what I'll look like?

"Thanks a bunch," said Kate when they had all her stuff stashed in one corner of her room. "Phew, I've got a lot of work to do right here."

"Like what?" Doug asked.

"I have to clear some space for the wedding presents. They'll start arriving as soon as word gets around. And if I know our mother, that won't take long," she said, chuckling.

As if by magic, a voice came floating up the stairs,

"Oh, Kate, I'm home! I have some sample invitations I want you to look at!"

"Be right down," Kate called. "See?"

She gave Doug a playful tap on the arm and headed downstairs.

Doug sat down on her bed and looked around. He couldn't imagine Kate's room filled with presents — wedding presents, at that.

He realized suddenly that he'd have to give her a present, too. Yeah, but how was he going to buy her anything? He poured all his money into video games and never had a spare cent.

The excitement of the wedding news was beginning to fade away. Doug got up and went downstairs. Mrs. Cannon and Kate were in the kitchen looking over the sample invitations.

He shuffled out the front door and sat down on the porch swing. It was still a while before dinner. If only he had some money he could play a few more games at the arcade before he had to sit down at the table with Kate, Terry, and this friend of his. A new guy around who was going to be a doctor.

He'll probably take a look at me and start talking about diets, he thought. Just what I don't want to hear. It's bad enough with Dad on his health kick!

Up until a year ago, Mr. Cannon had looked like an older version of Doug. But then something happened that, as he put it, "changed his outlook on life forever." Mr. Cannon had been rushed to the hospital with chest pains. Everyone was sure he was having a heart attack.

"We just have to hope for the best," Mrs. Cannon had said as she sat in the waiting room with Kate and Doug huddled next to her.

It turned out to be the best it could be — a very bad case of indigestion that acted a lot like a heart attack.

"You did the right thing coming in immediately, though," the doctor had said. Then he frowned and said, "In the shape he's in, he's lucky it wasn't something much, much worse."

Mr. Cannon had then undergone a complete physical. The result was a new way of life.

He began each morning with a regular routine of exercises. That was followed by a jog through the neighborhood. He constantly sang the praises of exercise, saying it helped overcome the "heavy genes" that ran in the family.

11

Next came breakfast. Mr. Cannon was on a strict diet — "Not for weight loss as much as health," he announced every morning as he ate his salt- and sugar-free cereal with skim milk.

And then, if Doug hadn't managed to have his own breakfast and get out of the kitchen, there was often a lecture on the healthy way of life. Maybe his father was right, but hearing it all the time drove Doug nuts. He didn't eat any more than his friends did, and he was usually too tired to exercise. His father's lectures ended up going in one ear and out the other.

Diet and exercise were the furthest things from Doug's mind right now as he rocked on the porch swing. The late afternoon sun beat down. Flies buzzed about and banged up against the screens. A gentle haze seemed to settle across Doug like a blanket. His eyelids drooped and finally closed.

Wheeeee-ew! Wheeeeee-ew! Wheeeee-ew!

A siren screeching in the distance jolted him awake.

It was the fire signal.

Doug jumped off the swing and ran down to the sidewalk. He gazed up and down the road. A dark

12

cloud of smoke rose high into the sky above the down-town area.

He hurried off toward it until he was stopped by the firefighter's blockade.

But there was no need to go farther. Even from there he could see the flames and smoke billowing out from doors and windows of the one building he knew better than any other. Just like a horrible nightmare come true, he watched as the raging fire consumed the video arcade.

It was going to be a long summer.

2

For Doug, the excitement of the fire was canceled out by the fact that his favorite hangout was burning to the ground. He couldn't wait to talk to his family about it. But when he got back from town, the news of the disaster died on his lips. Terry and Kate were out on the front porch with a tall, red-headed guy. He wore a gray T-shirt with his college colors on the sleeve, and it fit his trim, muscular body like a second skin.

"Hey, Doug," said Terry. "Kate said she told you about our getting married. Pretty cool, huh? This is my buddy, Red. You guys are both going to be in our wedding, so you might as well get to know each other."

"Uh, hi," said Doug, suddenly feeling like a lumpy sack of potatoes. He automatically sucked his stomach in.

14

"Nice to meet you, Doug," said Red, stretching out a hand.

Doug expected a crusher grip that would make him feel like a real weakling. But Red's handshake was firm without doing any damage.

Maybe he's not so tough, Doug thought. And as far as looking like one of those guys in the ads for health clubs, well, maybe he's just lucky and was born like that. Not like Dad with his "heavy genes," the same kind I probably have.

Then Kate and Terry began talking about places to go on a honeymoon. Doug was about to head into the house when Red turned to him and said, "I hear you're a hockey player. Goalie. That's a lot more work than people think."

"I guess," Doug agreed with a shrug. "They say you have to . . ."

For the next few minutes, they discussed some of the finer points of defensive hockey, until Mr. Cannon called out that dinner was ready.

Doug would have liked to keep on talking with Red, but the dinner conversation that night at the Cannon house was firmly fixed on the wedding. When Doug finally did get a word in, it was to tell them about the fire at the video arcade.

"That's too bad," said his father. "I hate to see any business hit so hard, but I'm sure they'll reopen eventually. Their insurance will pay for it. It'll be a while, though."

"Terry tells me that you're a real ace at video games, Doug," said Red. "That is, after he confessed how many times he lost to you over there."

Doug had to smile. Red Roberts was one of the friendliest guys he'd ever met. Terry, who was pretty sharp himself, sure knew how to pick his buddies.

Mrs. Cannon and Kate were talking about dresses and shoes while the guys kept up their own conversation at their end of the table.

Terry speared a piece of bright green asparagus from the serving bowl. "You're off to work bright and early tomorrow, Red, aren't you?"

"Are you working at the hospital?" asked Doug.

"Nope," said Red. "I'll be seeing enough of the not-so-great indoors soon enough. I'm spending the summer working on an outdoor project. But first, I have to find me a place to live."

"Red did it backwards," said Terry. "First he de-

16

cided he liked it here, then he got this terrific job, and now he's staying with me till he gets his own place. With my two brothers and three sisters, it's a little crowded at the Walcott homestead."

"Maybe we could help out. What about the carriage house?" asked Mrs. Cannon.

The carriage house stood at the beginning of the Cannons' driveway, close to the road. The Cannons had their carport made into a garage, and the carriage house was pretty much a storage barn now.

"It has that little place upstairs that carriage drivers lived in," Mrs. Cannon explained.

"Yes, there's electricity, and running water too," said Mr. Cannon. "Just needs to be turned on."

"And cleaned out," said Kate, wrinkling her nose. "Probably find all kinds of mementos up there. Phew!"

"Never mind," said Red. "Sounds real interesting to me. Can we take a look at it?"

"Sure, it's still light out," said Mr. Cannon.

"But first, how about some of this blueberry pie with a little vanilla ice cream?" suggested Mrs. Cannon. "Doug, here's yours." She handed him a heaping dish that threatened to topple over.

"I'll skip dessert, thank you," said Mr. Cannon.

Without looking up from his plate, Doug could feel his father's disapproving look bearing down on him as he shoveled in his pie and ice cream. It made him eat it all the faster.

After sighs of pleasure had been heard all around, a group of young people with blue mouths followed Mr. Cannon down to the carriage house.

It turned out to be in better condition than anyone thought.

"Won't take all that much work to whip it into shape," said Red.

"And you can use any of this old furniture we've been storing here," said Mr. Cannon.

Within a few minutes, it was agreed that Red could settle in as soon as they got the place cleaned out.

"I just have to check in at my job tomorrow morning. I'll be over in the afternoon to get started," said Red. "It shouldn't take more than a few good hours to clean up and move in."

"I'll help," said Doug. The words were out of his mouth before he knew it.

"That'd be great," said Red, flashing a big smile.

Why not? thought Doug. I don't have anything else to do. The arcade's burnt down and I'm tired of all my own video games. The guys are getting ready for camp. Might as well do something to kill time.

"Tell you what, Douglas," said Mrs. Cannon. "The two of us will pitch in and do what we can before Red gets back. We'll leave the heavy work to him."

The next day was Saturday. Under his mother's guidance, Doug swept out the small apartment, washed the windows, and carted off the trash that had accumulated.

"Well, it doesn't exactly shine," said Mrs. Cannon. "But it's a lot better than it was. Douglas, what do you say we have ourselves some lunch?"

"I'm famished," he said. "Could we go out to the new burger place on Main Street? They've got triple delishes."

"What on earth are triple delishes?" asked his mother.

"Three burgers in a four-part bun, with melted cheese, lettuce, tomato, mustard, mayo, and pickles," Doug chanted.

"If you can remember all that, you deserve to have one," said Mrs. Cannon, laughing. "I hope they have grilled chicken. Hmmmm, and while we're in town, I might as well talk to the florist so we can get started on wedding arrangements."

Doug's first thought was, Great, and I'll go over to the video arcade. And then he realized it was no longer there.

Oh, well, at least I have the triple delish to look forward to right now!

When they returned from lunch, Doug settled down on the porch swing and fell asleep. The triple delish had been followed by a chocolate sundae. The combination had filled him to bursting, and he'd practically rolled out of the car. Luckily, the owner of the flower shop had been out, so they'd come right home.

His afternoon slumber was shattered by a booming voice that called out, "Is this my fellow furniture mover?"

Doug looked up and saw Red standing next to the swing. "You bet!" he replied through a yawn. He got to his feet and followed Red down to the carriage house.

There wasn't a lot of furniture to be moved, but it took some effort. Doug was huffing and puffing after the first few minutes of exertion.

"Let's take a break," said Red, hefting a large over-stuffed chair to one side. Doug noticed that he wasn't even breathing hard.

"Yeah," muttered the younger boy. He settled down on the floor. There was an awkward silence broken only by the sound of his labored breathing. Embarrassed, he tried to think of something to say. He blurted out the first thing that came to mind.

"Hey, Red, how come you're in such good shape? Don't you spend a lot of time sitting around and studying? Don't tell me you're a big jock, too."

"I wouldn't call it that," said Red. "But I do like one sport, and I've put a lot into it."

"Oh, yeah?" asked Doug. "What's that?"

"Cycling," said Red.

"Riding a bicycle? That's a real sport?" Doug shook his head.

"You'd better believe it," said Red. "It's healthy, it's fun, but it can be very competitive, too."

"Did you ever compete? I mean, did you ever ride in a real race?" asked Doug.

"Uh-huh," said Red. "Come on, I want to show you something."

He led the way to what used to be a horse stall. Instead of a four-legged animal, there were three different bikes parked there now.

"Three bikes? What do you need three bikes for? They look pretty expensive," said Doug. He pictured his old three-speed gathering dust in the garage. He couldn't remember the last time he'd taken it out.

"That's because they're real sport bikes," said Red. "And one of them is just for serious racing."

"What's the big difference?" asked Doug with a shrug.

For the next few minutes, Red showed him the finer points of sport and racing bicycles.

"This is the one I use for just getting around," he said, indicating one with fat tires, fenders, and upright handlebars. "It's sort of an all-purpose model and the closest to the bikes you're probably used to. But this one has a lot more gears so it gets up hills easier."

"Would you use that in a race?" Doug asked.

"No, it's not made for that," Red explained. "These two are. First, here's my touring bike for road racing. See how thin the tires are and feel how light it is." He picked it up with one hand and passed it over to Doug.

"Wow, that *is* light!" said Doug, putting it down. "It looks like it has a million gears. How do you know which one to use?"

"It's not that hard," said Red. "Comes with practice."

"What about that one?" Doug asked. He nodded in the direction of a bike that looked even skinnier than the road racer. It had strange tires, too; each looked like a set of cymbals stuck together and rimmed with rubber.

"That's for racing on indoor tracks," said Red. "You wouldn't want to be out on the road on that baby."

"Why not?" Doug asked.

"Well, for one thing, it has no brakes." Red wheeled the indoor racer closer and knelt down. "And, see, it has no freewheel like the others. You can't coast on this bike. To keep moving ahead, you have to keep pedaling forward. If you want to stop, you start pedaling backward."

"Pedaling *backward*? You're kidding!" said Doug with disbelief. "I never realized there were so many different kinds of bikes — and different places to ride, I guess."

"And these are just a few," said Red. He wheeled the bikes back in line, then checked his watch. "Listen, I could go on and on, but I have something else I have to do."

"Like finish moving in?" Doug suggested.

23

"That's pretty much done," said Red. "No, I promised I'd put up some posters about that outdoor project I mentioned. We're looking for more volunteers to help out."

"I could show you some good places to put up the posters downtown," said Doug.

"That'd be great," said Red. "Let's go get your bike and we can start right out," said Red.

Doug was suddenly embarrassed.

"No, I'll run up and bring it back," Doug said hurriedly. "You wait here. It won't take a minute."

He rushed up the hill and ran into the kitchen. He found a wet sponge and some paper towels, then hurried into the garage and wiped the dust off his three-speed before coasting down the hill to the carriage house.

Red was seated on his all-purpose model, wearing a helmet.

"Here's one for you," he said, handing Doug the safety headgear.

"Thanks," said Doug. "I forgot mine, but I do have one. Slipped my mind."

"No sweat," said Red. "Let's go."

They pedaled out the driveway and down the road.

It took almost an hour to put up all of Red's posters. By that time, Doug was wiped out. The only thing he could think of was getting off his bike and sitting down to a drink of something very cold.

Red must have read his mind.

"Want to stop in there for something to drink?" he asked, pointing to an ice cream shop on the corner.

Doug nodded in great relief.

At this time of day, the place was almost empty. Doug and Red bought their drinks, then took them outside to some benches.

"You'd better have a big drink of water as well as that soda," said Red. "You look pretty hot. I don't want you to get dehydrated."

Doug could feel the perspiration sliding down his back under his shirt. The bike ride took a lot more effort than he'd thought it would.

"Yeah, I get pretty thirsty during the summer," he said. He got up and brought back two tall paper cups of water from the dispenser. "Here's one for you," he said.

"Thanks," said Red, taking a quick sip.

"So what exactly is this 'Rails to Trails' project we've been putting up posters for?" Doug asked.

25

Red unrolled one of the remaining announcements. "Like it says, we're cleaning up an old, abandoned railroad bed to make it into a path for recreation," Red replied.

"So people can go hiking along a nice, flat path?" asked Doug.

"That's one thing," said Red. "But it will also be used by bikers. It'll make a nice, safe place to go biking without worrying about cars and trucks and all that exhaust."

"Will it be used for races and stuff?" asked Doug. "I mean, you must be a big-shot racer, with all those bikes, huh?"

Red's face changed. His usual grin was now replaced by a set, serious expression. Instead of looking over at Doug, he was staring down into his cup of water.

Doug was afraid he'd said the wrong thing. "Was that dumb?" he asked. "You know, what I just said? I mean, I'm sorry if I —"

"Oh, no! No, don't worry. It's nothing to do with you," said Red quickly, looking up at Doug. "It's, well, you see, I'd better explain."

He settled back on the bench and told Doug about

26

the strong interest he'd had in cycling since he was a little kid.

"As a matter of fact, when I was real small and skinny, the kids used to called me 'Spokes,'" said Red, now laughing. "But I outgrew that, so don't get any wise ideas.

"Anyhow, I had this real passion, and my folks were great about it. They got me one bike after another, until, when I was about your age, I was using the finest amateur racing bikes around."

"Boy, you really liked it, didn't you!" said Doug. "How 'bout the other kids? You know, the guys you went to school with, and all that? Were they into bike riding, too?"

"Doug, you have to understand, *bike riding* is one thing and *cycling* is another," Red explained patiently. "Riding a bike is great, and pretty much anyone can do it. But cycling is a competitive *sport*. It's a whole different world. When you're in a race, it's just the bike, the road, and you, pulling for all you're worth."

"Oh," Doug said. Listening to Red made him realize how little he knew about sports outside of the ones offered at school. Because the school empha-

27

sized the importance of team playing, he had a choice of hockey, basketball, football, baseball, or soccer. He didn't mind playing on the teams — after all, he'd made some good friends, and besides, it was something the school required. He just didn't get into the competitive spirit like Pepper Meade and the others did. He guessed that was one reason he had decided not to go to summer hockey camp with them.

But Red was describing a whole different kind of sport — one that revolved around one's own abilities, not those of a team. You sank or swam on your own efforts, so if you didn't do well, you had no one to blame but yourself. And if you succeeded, the congratulations rested on your own shoulders.

What would that feel like, I wonder? Doug thought.

"Yup, it's a great sport, I can tell you that," said Red. "And for a while it was the most important thing in my life." He crushed his now-empty water cup and stood up. "Hey, but you haven't even said a word about the wedding. Are you glad your sister's getting married?"

Doug could tell Red wanted to change the subject. He went along with him and said, "Sure, I like Terry a lot. I just wish I had some money to buy them a really great present."

"Well, if you don't have money, you just have to get creative," said Red. "One of the coolest presents I ever got didn't even come in a box."

"What was it?" asked Doug.

"For my birthday one year, my godfather made a contribution in my name to a charity I really cared about. It made me feel great."

Yeah, but it still took some money, Doug thought. He didn't want Red to know that he was completely broke, so he decided it was time for *him* to change the subject now.

"Yup, those are really great bikes you have there. Get to race them much?" The question just popped out of his mouth.

"You know what?" said Red. "I think it's time we headed for home. Think you can make it back?"

It was obvious that racing wasn't a subject Red wanted to discuss. So Doug just nodded. He wasn't looking forward to climbing onto his old three-speed bike for the return trip. But he wasn't going to let Red know that now.

3

On the ride back, Doug noticed that Red was pacing himself so that they arrived back at the carriage house within moments of each other. The only difference was that Doug was huffing and puffing for all he was worth. Red got off his bike and looked as fresh as the morning breeze. Doug didn't want him to see how worn out he was, and luckily, Red didn't get a chance to notice.

There was a small group outside the carriage house waiting for them. Doug could see his folks, his sister, Terry, and a bunch of their friends. There were a few people Kate and Terry's age he didn't recognize. Probably friends from school, he guessed. They all looked happy and healthy, just like Kate and Terry — and Red.

"Hey, it's a housewarming party!" said Red.

"This guy is going to be one great doctor!" said Terry. "What powers of diagnosis!"

"Where have you been?" asked Kate. "Terry, get these guys something to eat and drink."

Mrs. Cannon had brought out some patio furniture and extra tables. Mr. Cannon was tossing lettuce leaves sprinkled with dressing into the air over a big salad bowl. There was also a buffet table already heaped with food that different people had brought. Doug could see some of his favorites: fried chicken, potato salad, baked beans, coleslaw. Over to one side there was a scooped-out watermelon with all kinds of fresh fruit in it. Right next to it were mounds of cookies and brownies, plus an assortment of pies.

It didn't take him long to dig right in. After draining a big glass of lemonade, he heaped a plate with a little of just about everything.

As he munched on a chicken leg, Doug heard Red talking to Kate. "Your brother's a pretty strong kid," he said. "I didn't think he could make it on that old three-speed, but he did fine."

"That's great," she said. "Did you tell him what a bike freak you are?"

"What a freak *I* am?" Red pointed his finger at her

31

and said, "You could be right up there with the champs."

Kate rolled her eyes to the sky. "I love riding for *fun* — and that's all."

"But you're a real fan," said Red. "You watch the races and check the results in the paper."

"Okay," said Kate. "I'll admit that — and nothing else. Anyhow, I'm glad you're getting to know my kid brother, since you're both going to be in the wedding party."

The wedding! There it was, thought Doug. It was just like some big mountain that had to be climbed. And there were two giant steps to be taken on the way to the top: he had to come up with a wedding present, and he'd probably have to squeeze into one of those penguin suits. He groaned at the thought of both.

Kate came over and sat down next to him.

"What's the matter, mopey?" she said. "Such a long face. Aren't you having fun?"

"Oh, sure," said Doug. He couldn't tell her what was really on his mind. "There just aren't a lot of kids my age around here."

"That's right," said Kate. "Mom said that most of

your gang was going off to hockey camp. How come you didn't go?"

"Just not interested," Doug mumbled, pushing a blob of ketchup around on his plate.

"So what are you going to be doing all summer?" she asked.

"Oh, I don't know," he said. "Helping out around the house, I suppose."

"Did I hear the word *help?*" asked Red, wandering over to where they were sitting.

"Uh-huh." Doug nodded.

"Doug's signed on as an all around house helper for the summer," Kate explained.

"Too bad he's stuck here," said Red. "We can use all the help we can get on our Rails to Trails project. We're always looking for volunteers. Maybe you could give us some of your time now and then, Doug."

Mrs. Cannon had overheard this part of the conversation.

"I've heard something about that project. It's going to connect Lakeridge to two other towns. And I think it'll pass close by your middle school, Doug."

"That sounds like a good idea to me," his father

said. "You'd probably go stir-crazy just hanging around here all the time, Douglas, wouldn't you? And, working outside will give you an opportunity to get some real exercise."

Doug had trouble keeping from groaning. Leave it to Dad to find a way to lecture him! Why should he go off and work on some dumb project anyhow? "What could *I* do to help?" he asked. "I can't use a chainsaw or anything like that, yet."

"Oh, there are plenty of little jobs that don't require using power equipment," said Red. "Sometimes it's great just to have someone around to deal with the small stuff."

"If you really think so,"said Doug. "But how would I get there?"

"By bike," said Red. "It's not that much farther than the ride we took today."

Doug remembered the pounding of his heart when he'd finally reached the carriage house. He wasn't so sure he was up for a regular workout like that.

"Oh, and I can drive him over once in a while,"said Mrs. Cannon.

"Or I can," said Kate.

"And I'm sure his father can pick him up if one of us can't," said Mrs. Cannon.

"Of course," Mr. Cannon said. "Although I think the biking idea is the best."

"So, it looks like it's settled," said Red. "Okay, Doug?"

"Well, I guess so," he said. "When would I start?"

"Monday," said Red. "First thing in the morning."

Doug sighed. He looked over to where his bike was parked. He'd never realized how much it looked like an instrument of torture.

The bike trip to the Rails to Trails project wasn't quite as bad as Doug had imagined it would be. Luckily, the last part was on a flat stretch of reclaimed railroad bed that provided for a nice, smooth ride.

When they got there, Red introduced Doug all around.

One woman, who said her name was Sally, handed him an orange T-shirt with RAILS TO TRAILS in big green letters on the front. A lot of the others were wearing them. Doug went to put his on, but it didn't fit. He looked at the label. It said "Large," but he knew it was too small for him. He hung it over his handlebars and put his own T-shirt back on.

Most of the workers were Red's age or older. Doug thought he'd be the youngest person on the job. Then he spotted another kid who looked about his age leaning against one of the trucks. He was tall and skinny, with pale skin and jet-black hair that flopped over his forehead.

There was no time to find out who he was, though. People had started unloading equipment and it looked as though work would begin right away.

Doug was starting to feel a little weak in the knees about joining up with this group, when he noticed the open back of a station wagon to one side. In between the people who partially blocked his view, Doug could see a coffee urn and cartons of what had to be doughnuts.

"That's for later, when we get hungry," said Red, following his gaze. "Right now, there's work to be done. How about giving me a hand carrying these tools?"

For the next hour, Doug stayed pretty close to Red. He handed him tools and fetched small pieces of equipment, and once he went over to the open station wagon to bring him back a tall cup filled with plain old water. A whiff of doughnuts made his stomach rumble, but he tried to ignore it.

The tall, skinny kid was chugalugging a drink from a big thermal cup. He wiped his mouth with the back of his hand and looked over at Doug.

"Hi, I'm Billy Torrant," he said.

"Doug Cannon."

"Ya get real thirsty out here, huh?" said Billy.

"Yeah," Doug answered. "You been on the job here long?"

"No, I only moved into town a little while ago. This is my first day," said Billy.

"Me, too," said Doug, brightening at the discovery he wasn't the only newcomer.

"Yeah," said Billy. "I'm here 'cause my folks think I should toughen up. I eat okay, but I'm still kind of skinny. They're worried that when I start school, the other kids will poke fun at me — like some of them did where we used to live. They wanted me to go to some fitness camp this summer, but I couldn't because of the move. And then they saw one of those posters and thought I might get some exercise working on this project."

"That could have been one of the posters I helped to put up," said Doug.

"Hey, Doug, you got that drink? I'm parched!" came Red's voice from down the track.

As the next hour passed, Doug got to know a few of the other men and women working on the project.

He found himself helping them as much as Red.

Suddenly, someone shouted, "Coffee time!" and work fizzled away as the midmorning break started.

Doug got himself a small container of milk and a jelly doughnut. He went over to where he and Red had parked their bikes in a shady spot and flopped down. Red was already there. He held a Thermos to his mouth and took a long, deep drink.

"Do you bring your own coffee?" Doug asked.

"No, it's a kind of herbal tea I like," said Red. "I'm not much into coffee and regular tea." He crunched on a big red apple he'd produced from his knapsack.

Doug's doughnut suddenly seemed soggy and unappetizing. After two mouthfuls, he put it aside. Without a word, Red fumbled into his knapsack, pulled out a second apple, and offered it to Doug. Doug hesitated, then accepted it.

There was so much about Red that Doug didn't

know. Every time he turned around, there seemed to be something new. But the one thing Doug was most curious about didn't seem to be something Red liked to talk about: why he'd stopped racing.

There was a long silence between them.

"Okay, you want to know why I gave up cycling, right?" Red asked.

Was he a mind reader? Doug wondered.

"It's not that big a deal," Red went on. "But it was at the time. See, I had really fallen in love with it. There was nothing else in the world I wanted to do. So I decided I'd go the amateur route and then eventually turn pro."

"Really?" asked Doug. "How far did you get?

"Pretty darn close," said Red. "I'd won a lot of races as an amateur and even came close in a few international ones." He took a final bite of apple and chewed.

"What I really wanted was to compete in the Olympics. Yeah, I dreamt of winning that gold medal all the time. My training was pretty well concentrated on just one event: the individual pursuit. But it didn't work out. I wasn't good enough the first time I tried to qualify." Red had a distant look in his eyes. Doug held his breath, waiting for him to go on.

"Anyway, by the time the next Olympics rolled around four years later, I had gone pro. In fact, when your sister first met me, she recognized me from a newspaper picture. I was holding a cup I had won. Funny," he added. "That was the last race I ever competed in."

"Your last race! Hey, what made you stop racing?"

"I had an accident."

"A bad one? During the race?"

"Yes, to both questions," said Red. "I made a dumb mistake on a turn and took out several others. But I was the only one seriously hurt."

"Did you finish the race?" Doug asked.

"I couldn't," said Red. "They took me off in an ambulance. I'd broken my leg in several places and was laid up for a long time."

"But you ride fine now," said Doug. "So you must have gotten completely better, right?"

"Not exactly," said Red. "My body no longer has that real competitive edge. I can still ride in simple races, as long as I don't push it too hard. In fact, I still belong to the Lakeridge Cycling Club." He stood up, stretched, and looked down at Doug. "You know, I've always wondered what would have happened if I'd had my chance in the Olympics. Even when I was on the pro circuit, the dream of racing in them stayed with me. But any thoughts I ever had about the Olympics, well, since the accident I've had to put them out of my mind."

Doug didn't know what to say. He just sat there and stared at the ground. It had to have been terrible for Red to lose the one thing he wanted most: a shot at the Olympics.

"Hey, it's not the end of the world," said Red. "Cycling's loss could just be medicine's great gain. Maybe I'll discover a cure for the common cold."

"Maybe you'll get up off your duff and help us haul this load over the track," said Jimmy Bannister, a bearlike man who served as the work crew leader. Despite his gruff tone, he was good-natured and everyone liked him.

"Yes, sir, mister boss," said Red, with a mocking tone to his voice. "Anything you say. Come on, Doug, and give us a hand."

For the rest of the day, Doug pitched in wherever he could. He soon discovered that he wasn't being asked to do much real work. It looked as though the regulars didn't think he had the strength it took to do

41

a lot of the jobs. He ended up clearing the small brush and helping drag it out of the way. But he never was asked to lend a hand on any of the big jobs.

Not so with Billy, he noticed. Once in a while they worked together on the small stuff. But Billy's height made him a natural for getting at some tall chores without a ladder. A couple of times, just when the two of them started to talk, Billy got called away to do just that.

Work was still work, though, and Doug hadn't done this much in a long, long time. Toward the end of the day, he had no energy left at all. He gradually drifted into the background until he found a cool spot where he could settle down out of sight. He leaned back against the trunk of a tree and within seconds was sound asleep.

In his slumber, a picture began to form. At first, it was just a dim sound, like a buzz. Then it grew bigger and bigger until it was a roar. Bright lights broke through and brought into focus the figure of a boy on a bicycle. It was boy without a face, but he was about Doug's age and height. He looked a lot thinner and tougher as he pedaled forward furiously, coming right into the center of Doug's vision. The noise became the roar of a crowd. They were shouting "Cannon! Can-non!" Flowers were being thrown at the boy on the bicycle and eventually a gold crown settled on his head. Suddenly, the five colored rings of the Olympics rose up in front of him and a ribbon with a gold medal was tied around his neck by a pair of mysterious hands.

"You've earned this," said a voice from the crowd.

Doug blinked his eyes open. The voice belonged to Red, who was standing next to him. He was holding out an ice cream on a stick.

"I must have dozed off," said Doug, scrambling up awkwardly. He took the ice cream from Red and bit into it without hesitation.

"Just as well," said Red. "You put in one heckuva day for your first one on the job."

"I'll do even better tomorrow," said Doug around a mouthful.

"Nope, tomorrow your Mom told me she has work planned for you at home," said Red. "Besides, we don't want to wear you out all at once. And, hey, I've got a surprise for you. Jimmy's going right by your

43

house, so he'll drop you and your bike off. You can throw it in the back of his pickup. Sally suggested it. She thought you looked wiped out."

Suddenly the ice cream lost its flavor. Sally thinks I'm a wuss! Doug thought, his face turning a dull red. I suppose Red and Billy and everyone else does, too. Can't finish the job. Can't even ride my bike back home. Well, I'll show them.

"Tell Jimmy I don't need him," said Doug angrily. He stomped over to his bike, slapped on his helmet, and climbed into the seat. "Just because I'm fat doesn't mean I'm weak!"

"Doug, nobody thinks that!" said Red. "Jimmy only offered —"

"I'm fine," shouted Doug over his shoulder. "I don't need anyone's help."

His chubby legs pumped as he headed down the track. In a few seconds he was beyond the sound of Red's voice.

4

Beads of sweat rolled down from Doug's forehead as he pedaled furiously along the restored track. His muscles ached and his body hurt in other ways, too. The back of his neck flamed where he'd gotten sunburned. His arms stung from where he'd scratched at a zillon insect bites, and his right thumb had a sliver in it he couldn't pick out.

But despite these pains, he'd been enjoying himself. He'd felt appreciated. That was before the dream and Red's waking him up to say Jimmy would drive him home. Now he just felt humiliated. Well, he'd show them.

The track was longer than he thought, and he was already breathing hard before he'd gone halfway. Just keep pedaling, he told himself. All you have to do is get home and you'll be okay.

But what about Red? And Sally? Were they back there talking about him? Were they laughing at him because he couldn't do the tough jobs?

The more he thought about it, the sorrier he felt for himself, and the harder he pumped. And the more the sweat poured down across his face. It oozed into the corners of his eyes and mixed with the tears that he couldn't keep from coming.

He could barely see when he came to the end of the track. Instead of slowing down for the turn, he went zooming ahead into the brush. The front wheel of his bike sank into the soft ground and skewed to one side, dragging the handlebars with it. Doug held on for a moment, then lost his balance and tumbled down into the scratchy undergrowth.

He sat still, afraid to move for a moment. His legs were tangled up in the frame and twisted front wheel. If he could wiggle them free, he'd be all right. He was reaching over to straighten out the handlebars when he felt a sharp pain in his arm. He'd been so worried about breaking a leg, he hadn't even noticed the blood pouring out of a cut just below his elbow. When he did, his vision swam.

Okay, I know what to do, he said to himself. First of

all, stay cool. Then, I just squeeze my arm a little bit above where it's cut. Now I add some more pressure, raise my arm above my heart, and it should slow the bleeding.

He was so busy applying first aid to his cut arm, he didn't hear the sound of other riders approaching. But before he knew it, there was Red with Andy Potts and Tommy Lopardo, two other members of the work crew, coming toward him.

"What happened?" Red asked, kneeling down next to Doug.

"Must have been something on the track and I skidded," said Doug.

He hardly noticed Red glancing over his shoulder to look for skid marks that weren't there.

"Let's take a look at that arm," Red said. "Tommy, grab the first aid kit out of my backpack." He asked Doug a lot of questions about whether or not he felt pain anywhere else. When Doug assured him he didn't, Red called out, "Hey guys, want to give me a hand getting him out of here?"

Slowly and carefully, they untangled Doug's legs from the wreckage of his bike. The pain in his arm had turned into a dull throb, and he was able to assist them in getting him to his feet. But when he was standing, he felt a little woozy.

"Here, you just sit down under this tree," said Red. "I'm not trying to play doctor, Doug, but I don't think you did too much damage. Guys, his house is just a few minutes away. I'm going to ride over and see if someone can pick him up in a car. I'll be right back."

"What about my bike?" Doug called as Red pedaled away.

Tommy shook his head. "The frame is bent real bad. Looks like you may have totaled it."

When Mrs. Cannon arrived, she insisted that a doctor look at Doug's injuries. So over his protests, she drove him to the clinic, which was open late that day. The doctor confirmed that the cut wasn't serious.

"But there's always a chance of infection," he said. "I'd better give you a shot and some follow-up medication. Then I'll put on a clean, new bandage."

When they got back, Red was up at the house sitting on the front steps with Kate and Terry.

"We heard about the crash," said Kate. "Too bad about your bike. How's the arm?"

49

"Doc says I may never play the violin again," Doug said sadly.

"Wait a minute," Terry piped up. "You can't play the violin now!"

Mrs. Cannon shook her head at their nonsense. "He'll be fine in a few days. The cut didn't go all that deep."

"Look at that," said Kate. "One day on the job and already my brother's on sick leave. Who said this kid isn't sharp as a tack?"

Their good-natured banter made Doug feel a whole lot better. In fact, for a few moments he forgot all about the accident — and what caused it.

The next evening, long after dinner was finished and Doug was sitting out on the porch swing looking at a catalog of video games, Mr. Cannon came over and sat down next to him.

"I had a talk with Red a little while ago," he said. "He told me he was quite impressed with your first day on the job yesterday. Everyone was."

Doug was silent.

His father continued, "In fact, he told me that he

50

was sure they would appreciate your coming back as soon as possible."

Doug shrugged his shoulders. He waited for the "working in the outdoors is good for your health" lecture to start. To his surprise, it didn't.

"But your bike is beyond repair. I had the fellows over at the garage take a look at it. So if you're going to continue with the project, you'll need a new way of getting back and forth to the site."

"I guess I'll have to wait until someone drives me," said Doug, staring at the porch floor.

"Well, there might be another way," said Mr. Cannon.

"Oh, yeah? What?" asked Doug suspiciously.

"You *could* pedal your way back and forth if you had a new bike," said his father. Doug looked up quickly. Mr. Cannon grinned. "As a matter of fact, I just got one for you."

"You did!"

"Uh-huh, a new twelve-speed racing bike. Red helped me pick it out for you," said Mr. Cannon. "It's tagged with your name on it at the bike store in the mall. If you like it, it's yours."

Doug was stunned. "But, wait a minute, it's not my birthday for a long time. And Christmas is way off. How come?"

"Well, I've been doing some thinking. You know all that exercise equipment I bought when I got home from the hospital?"

"You mean that junk sitting down in the basement? The stuff Mom wants you to use or get rid of?"

"Yes, well, I finally did," said Mr. Cannon. "I sold it — and put the money toward your bike."

"But you said you *might* use it again someday," said Doug.

"There's a reason that stuff's been collecting dust downstairs. It just didn't work for me. My morning jog and a set of dumbbells are all I need. Although Red tells me a muzzle might be a good addition, too." Mr. Cannon laughed at Doug's confused expression. "It seems I've become something of a monster, preaching about good health and the wonders of exercise to anyone within earshot. Especially to you. Red politely told me that, in his experience, the decision to lead a healthy life can't be made for you. You have to decide to do it for yourself."

He laid a hand on Doug's shoulder and looked him

52

in the eye. "So that was my last lecture. From now on, no more. If you want the bike, then it's yours. Let's call it a member of the wedding party present. You could be pressed into wedding messenger and errand service, you know. But however you use it, I trust you'll do it safely and wisely."

"But a twelve-speed," said Doug. "That's stupendous. And a racing bike. Wow! It's a lot more than I need for errands."

"Well, let's say Red had something to do with it, too. He convinced me that it could be a good investment," said Mr. Cannon.

Doug jumped up and threw his arms around his father, wincing slightly when his left one made contact. "Thanks, Dad, you're the greatest. Hey, Mom," he called into the house. "Can we go to the mall first thing tomorrow morning?"

Mrs. Cannon had some wedding errands to do, so she agreed to his request. The next day they were at the bike shop bright and early.

Doug was amazed at the model Red had picked out. It was everything he had ever heard about — and then some. In fact, at first, he was a little taken aback.

"I don't know, Mom," he said. "It's a lot more bike than I imagined. I don't know if I'll ever be able to learn to ride it."

It seemed so lightweight. Would it be strong enough to hold him? That's what really had him worried. But he decided it was worth a try. So, along with a box of accessories Red had selected, they loaded the bike into the car and drove home.

On the way, Doug told his mother that he really was a little nervous about trying it out.

"Red seemed to think you'd do fine," she said. "In fact, this morning before he left for work he stopped by while you were still upstairs. He told me that he'd help you put it all together and give you some pointers if you could wait until he has a little free time."

"Well, I won't be riding it until the bandage comes off," said Doug. "That gives us a little time."

Doug was silent for the rest of the ride. For the first time since his little spill, he thought back to everything that had happened on Monday. In the midst of it all, he remembered the dream. He could almost hear the sound of the crowd shouting, "Can-non! Can-non!"

Oh, sure, he thought. The van jostled over a bump and Doug felt his gut jiggle. Right, I'm going to be in the Olympics. Yeah, tell me another!

Still, looking at his new bike, Doug let the image of his dream linger for a bit.

On Saturday morning, Red came up the driveway with a toolbox in hand. Mr. Cannon called out to him, "Okay, let's see what we have here. Doug, time to put all the bells and whistles on that new bike of yours."

"Let's go," said Doug. He brought out the box of accessories.

"Okay, let's start with that package of toe clips," said Red. "Believe me, once you get used to riding with those on, you won't believe what a difference it makes."

As each part was added — the clip-on pump, fancy aerobar attachments, water bottle — Red pointed out how it was all part of cycling.

Then came something that looked a little like an old-fashioned saddlebag, only a lot smaller.

"It's called a pannier," said Red. "Your dad insisted that we get a good one."

"Remember I told you that there might be errands to run on this bike?" said Mr. Cannon with a smile.

"Well, this is how you'll do some of the carrying. In fact, I think you'll find — no, never mind."

"What, Dad? What were you going to say?" asked Doug.

"Just a little lecture I'm not going to deliver," said Mr. Cannon, smiling. "Old habits die hard."

And new ones are hard to learn, thought Doug, staring at the shiny new bike.

The bandage came off in a few more days. By that time, Doug had become familiar with all the parts of his new bike.

"Now comes the big test," said Red one evening. "Riding it. You sure your arm doesn't bother you?"

"Nope."

"You're not worried that you're going to have another accident, are you?" Red asked.

"I thought about it," said Doug. "I figure that accidents just happen whether you want them to or not. But if I do things right, my chances are a lot better. So I want to learn to ride this bike right."

"Okay, you've got the right attitude," said Red. "Let's get started. The most important thing is making sure you and the bike fit one another. That means

56

making a few adjustments. We'll start with the saddle."

"You mean the seat?"

"On racing bikes, like this one, it's called the saddle," said Red with a smile. "Your cycling education is just beginning."

It took a lot longer than Doug ever thought it would. When the saddle was the right height, the drop handlebars felt funny. He wobbled when he tried to sit erect and hold on to them.

"Lean into them," said Red. "About forty-five percent of your weight should be over those handlebars. That takes a lot more stress off your lower back."

Doug wiggled around, trying to get more comfortable. The inside of his thighs began to ache. His hands were sweating and sliding on the handlebar grips.

"Don't worry, we'll get you mitts," said Red. "And I think those jeans may have to go. Too much danger of their getting caught somewhere."

Doug balked. Oh, no, he's going to make me wear those skintight biker things! I'll look like a big, colored sausage!

"Since it's summertime, you can start off with a

simple pair of shorts," said Red, much to Doug's re-lief.

"Hey, bikers of this world, anybody care for a lem-onade break?" asked Mrs. Cannon, wandering into their practice area next to the carriage house. They had just finished pedaling around the driveway for the fifth time.

"Would I ever!" said Doug. He hopped off the bike, then carefully leaned it against the fence. "I feel like I just got down off a mountain!"

And it's just beginning, he realized. He hadn't even learned to shift gears yet! For a quick moment, he began to wonder if having this racer was such a good idea. He was starting to see that it came with a lot of responsibility.

As they stood there sipping slowly on the cool lem-onade, Red said, "You're doing just fine. But it'll be different when you get out on the open road. I think we ought to knock it off for now. It's starting to get dark and there isn't enough time to go over road tech-niques."

"Is there that much of a difference? I mean, is it always like a race?" Doug asked.

"No, it's just — well, wait until I get a little more

58

time," said Red. "Tell you what, I know a good side road that has a dead end. We'll go over there and practice tomorrow. Okay?"

"Okay," said Doug. He drained his lemonade glass and looked over at Red. "Could we just give it one more trip around the carriage house, up the driveway, and back?"

"Why not?" said the older biker. "Maybe that will tire you out so we can all get some rest!"

Mrs. Cannon smiled in agreement.

5

The Cannons got their rest that night. Doug hadn't realized how much exertion he'd put into his bike training. When he hit his bed, he barely moved until morning.

In fact, he slept a little later than usual. By the time he got up, Red had already left for work on the railbed. Doug hadn't been back since the accident, and he was sorry to miss the chance to ride over on his new bike. But he knew that it wouldn't be a smart thing to do on his own — at least until he'd had some road training.

So that afternoon, the minute Red got back, Doug was down at the carriage house waiting for him.

"So, when do we go over to that dead-end street to practice?" asked Doug.

"What kind of a monster have I created?" said Red,

shaking his head. "Okay, but first, you really have to know how to shift gears. It's a lot different from your three-speed." Red spent about fifteen minutes with him going over the workings of the twelve-speed system. When he was satisfied that Doug had it under control, he gave him a thumbs-up sign. "Now give me a second to get cleaned up," he said.

They borrowed the Cannons' van, loaded their bikes in it, and set off.

"I have a little surprise for you," said Red. "Remember the tall boy who was working with us on the Rails to Trails project?"

"Billy Torrant?"

"That's him," said Red. "Well, his street is the dead-ender I told you about. Seems he wants to learn more about cycling, too. We'll meet up with him there."

Doug wasn't so sure he wanted someone his own age around to see him wobbling along on his new bike. But Billy seemed pretty friendly. Maybe it wouldn't be too bad.

When he saw Billy and his bike, Doug immediately felt better. His bike was okay, but not half as nice as Doug's. And Billy seemed just as friendly as before, greeting their arrival with an enthusiastic wave.

"Hey, Billy, how's it going?" Doug called over to him.

Billy pedaled over. Even on the bike, he seemed about a foot taller than anyone else.

"Pretty good," said Billy. "I'm just a little worried I'm not going to be any good at this."

"That makes two of us," said Doug. He was glad Billy felt the same.

"Okay, you guys," said Red. "Let's see where the problems are. Doug, just take a ride down to the end of the road, turn, and come back. Then Billy, when he starts his turn, you take off and do the same. I'll talk to you both when you get back."

For the next half hour, Red carefully pointed out what they were doing right and wrong. He showed them how to settle into a comfortable riding position, but one that would still give them control.

"Use the toe clips to do some of the work," he reminded Doug.

Doug nodded in agreement.

"Less tension on your grip," he shouted at Billy.

Billy's head bobbed up and down.

"All right, you're both ready for a little ride around

the block," he finally announced. "But before we hit the road, let's do a safety check."

He reminded Doug that this bike was a lot more responsive than his old one. There would be a temptation for both boys to try all sorts of hotdog maneuvers. That was the absolute worst thing they could do — a sure invitation to disaster.

Thoroughly warned, Doug climbed up onto the saddle and slipped his feet into the toe clips until the toes of his shoes hit the ends. He buckled the strap on his helmet and grabbed the handlebars.

"Comfortable?" asked Red.

"Uh-huh,"said Doug.

"Billy, you all set, too?" Red asked.

Billy looked over and said, "Yup."

"Okay, here we go," said Red. "Remember, stay behind me and just follow what I do as best you can. We're only going for a short run around the block for now. If there's time, we'll try a little longer distance afterward."

It seemed to Doug that the trip took no time at all. Wow, he thought, if it's that easy, racing must be a breeze.

"How did it feel?" asked Red, dismounting.

"Great! Let's go, I want to do a longer trip this time," said Doug.

"Not so fast," said Red. "Let's talk over what you did wrong."

"Wrong? Did we do something wrong?" asked Doug.

"What about pulling up alongside me at the first stop?" asked Red. "I told you to stay behind."

"I don't see what the big deal about that is," said Doug.

"It's not all that bad in itself," said Red. "But if you were in a race and you didn't follow the plan laid out by your team, then it would be."

"But we weren't in a race," said Billy.

Red paused, then nodded. "You're right. I guess I have race discipline so firmly in my head, I judge everything by that standard. Listen, you guys, I've had a long day and I'm really bushed. Why don't we call it quits for now." He walked off toward the van and slid open the door.

Billy called over after him. "Hey, thanks a lot for coming over and giving me all those pointers." He turned to Doug. "Maybe we can get together and practice some time."

"Sure," said Doug. "I'd like that. But I'd better help load up the van now." Doug watched as Red lifted his bike into the van. Red looked as though he were lost in a dream.

Back up at his house, Doug was greeted by the sight of Kate swirling about in a cloud of white, gauzy material. Mrs. Cannon stood by admiring her.

"It's going to be my veil," said Kate. "Won't it be fabulous?"

"Sure," he said. "Terrific."

Doug had never realized that there was so much stuff involved in planning a wedding. He'd been to a few and he remembered the ceremony and the reception. There was always a ton of food as far as he could tell. He figured that's what took all the time. But not so with Kate's wedding. There were a million other details everyone talked about.

Even so, during the last few days he had just about put the wedding out of his mind. The only time it broke through was when someone said, "We'll have to make sure you have a pair of plain black shoes, Doug," or "Won't be long before you have to get fitted for your tuxedo, Doug." Every mention brought a stab of anxiety to his stomach.

The other reminder of his wedding woes was the constant stream of wedding gifts that kept arriving. It seemed like everyone he'd ever heard about — even crazy Aunt Sally, whom he'd never even seen — had sent something. Everyone, that is, but her own brother. He still hadn't figured out how he was going to come up with a gift.

All in all, he almost wished there wasn't going to be any wedding. But Kate was so happy all the time, how could he even think of something like that? So that night after dinner, he sat down all by himself at the kitchen table. Look, he reasoned, since this wedding isn't going to go away, I've really got to figure out what I can do about it. I've got to come up with something to give her!

"Jimmy, want to move that truck a little closer to this pile?" called out Red. "Hey, look who's finally back on the job? Doug, you're just in time to help us load this brush."

There were greetings from the other guys on the work crew as Doug pitched right in with them. Less then ten days after his little spill, he'd found himself itching for some activity.

That's the only itching I'm going to do, he said to himself as he packed his pannier with insect repellent. He also threw in some sunblock — no more sunburn, either — and a pair of work gloves like the older guys wore. He checked to make sure his water bottle was full, too.

The one thing he didn't take with him was that T-shirt he'd been given. He'd tried it on again and it still fit him like a sausage skin. But at least he'd gotten it on this time. Maybe it would stretch, he told himself.

Doug hadn't started out with Red first thing that morning. Instead, he'd wanted to ride over on his new bike all by himself. He'd been practicing with Billy and out on the open road with Red several times, and he felt confident enough to go it on his own. If all went well, he planned to talk to Red about an idea he had.

When the crew finally broke for lunch, Doug steered Red off to a quiet spot where they could sit and talk.

"I need to talk to you about something," said Doug.

"Sure, sport," said Red. "Anything I can do?"

"I want to find out more about cycling — and racing. I mean, more than just goofing off around the neighborhood or riding back and forth to work," said Doug.

"Doesn't seem like too tall an order," Red said. "But any particular reason why?"

"Well, you know my new bike was a real special present from my dad. I'd like to get so good at riding that he'd be proud of me," said Doug. He avoided looking at Red as he continued. "Maybe I could even enter some little race or something. What do you think?"

Red was quiet for a moment. Then he said, "I think your father has one great son."

Doug flushed, embarrassed but pleased by the praise.

"Yeah, okay, but the problem is, see, I don't know how to really ride well enough and how to get into a race or anything like that. So, maybe you could, you know, help me out?"

"Son of a gun!" said Red with a strangely wicked smile. "Tell you what, this weekend there's an open house at my old cycling club. We can go over and take a look around. What do you say to that?"

"The Lakeridge Cycling Club you talked about before?" said Doug. "But isn't that some kind of hotshot racing club?"

"It is one of the best, but I think you'll find out that it's also a great place to learn about cycling."

"Okay, sounds good to me," said Doug. "Saturday? You're sure you don't mind?"

"It's either that or clean my little apartment," Red replied. "So?"

"Saturday it is," said Doug enthusiastically.

And Saturday morning it was, when Doug followed Red in a leisurely ride across town to the club. He wondered what it would look like.

It turned out to be a square red-brick building that had once been a garage.

As they pulled up in front of it, Doug could see a bunch of people standing around talking next to their bikes. They were all decked out in sleek, skintight racing gear. Every one of them seemed to have a muscular, taut body without a spare ounce of flesh. There was no one who looked remotely his age. Or his size.

His heart sank.

6

"Come on, I'll show you around," said Red.

Doug was about to suggest that maybe his being there wasn't such a good idea when a few other kids about his age came around the corner of the building. And, he was happy to see, they were pretty much dressed just as he was, in shorts and T-shirts. With a few exceptions, none of them had the special shoes and skintight shirts and shorts that the older people were wearing.

"This is our library," said Red with a mocking tone as he pointed to a bookcase filled to bursting with a collection of books, magazines, and pamphlets. "Cycling's growing so fast, we get a ton of stuff sent to us in the mail. But the important news is on the bulletin board over here." He pointed to a big cork board next to the entrance to the meeting room. It was covered with notices of cycling events, safety warnings, a few newspaper pictures of members flashing winning smiles.

Doug wandered over and took a look at some of the notices. He quickly scanned the board for anything that might appeal to beginners. There were a few things he decided he'd look into later. Then, in the upper right corner, he saw the famous five-ring symbol of the Olympics. He was still staring at it when Red called him into the meeting room.

"Jack Millman is the president of the club," he explained. "He's going to talk about how we operate and then open up the floor to questions."

As they took their seats, a lot of people came up and said a few words to Red. It was obvious that he was one of the most popular members of the club.

Just before the talk began, he saw Billy Torrant come in and take a seat in the back row. Darn it, he thought, I wish I'd told him I was coming.

Doug settled in for the talk, which was mostly about membership dues, forthcoming events, and what the club offered in training — nothing that really impressed him that much. By the end of the talk, he'd pretty much decided that he'd be better off getting into cycling on his own. This group was too slick for him.

Then came the question-and-answer session. The first question came from Billy.

"Yuh, I'm Billy Torrant," he said, "And I'm sort of a newcomer in town as well as in cycling. It doesn't sound to me like there's a lot here for those of us just starting out."

Doug could hardly believe what he was hearing. Other than the part about being new in town, it was exactly what he'd been thinking.

Jack Millman explained that the club had just put together a real basic, start-from-scratch, nuts-and-bolts program for new racers. In fact, the leader of that program was in the audience and he wanted to introduce him.

"Will Red Roberts please stand up?" he said.

As Red got to his feet, Doug almost fell off his chair in surprise. Then Red's "Son of a gun!" and wicked smile from the other day popped right back into his mind. When Red sat back down, Doug grinned at him and nodded knowingly. Red grinned back.

After a few more questions, Jack Millman made a final announcement.

"I just want to let everyone know that the Lake-ridge Cycling Club is also going to be holding our own event in the near future. That's right, we're working on putting together the Tour de Lakeridge. We'll let you know when we have all the details worked out."

Doug applauded politely with everyone else, then joined Billy and a few other kids heading in Red's direction.

"Okay," said Red. "We'll start regular training this coming Monday, but first we have to get down to some basics. That means your bikes, to begin with. Let's go take a look and see what we have."

Doug followed the group of about a dozen kids out to the front of the club, where their bikes were parked. He listened as Red went over each bike with its owner, pointing out the good parts and then the problems. Red's once-over of his bike took no time. He just told everyone that it was a good, sturdy, well-constructed bike that would probably serve a long time before its owner moved on to a fancier model.

Doug wasn't all that sure that he would last long enough in cycling for such a move, but he didn't say anything.

"Okay, come on back inside," said Red. "We have

some more things to talk about before we go for a short test ride."

When they were all settled in one section of the meeting room, Red made an announcement.

"We have to talk about clothing," he stated.

That was greeted with audible groans from the group.

Doug smiled to himself: At least I'm not the only one in this pickle.

Red started from the bottom up.

"The bad news," he informed the group, "is that you're all going to have to wear proper cycling shoes. Sneakers just don't work. They don't slip in and out of your toe clips easily and they're too flexible. You waste a lot of energy in that flex. Plus, believe it or not, they're too heavy. Cycling shoes are designed for just what they do best. Hey, you wouldn't play basketball in combat boots, would you?"

That made the group laugh and lightened things up a little.

"Next, you all might think you look real cool in your shorts and tank tops, but mark my words, you're not going to be all that happy when you start cycling for any real distances."

74

By the time he got through explaining the cons of the wrong clothes and the pros of the right kind, everyone in the group was convinced that they should go along with Red's recommendations.

"I don't expect everyone to be suited up right the first week," Red added. "But by week number two or three I think it would be a good idea."

Doug overheard two girls discussing buying outfits. "Well, at least they won't be bulky like that ski stuff we bought last winter!" one of them giggled.

Yeah, they're skintight, thought Doug. Well, if that's what it takes to get going. I guess I'll have to do it.

"Now, let's go hit the road for a little practice run," said Red. "I'll lead off and stay in front for the first half. When we start heading back here, I'll drop to the rear and pull up alongside you just to see how you're doing. It's not going to be a very long trip, so don't worry about being in shape for it. We'll get into that on Monday, too."

The group followed Red back outside and over to the bike rack. Doug put on his helmet and climbed on his bike. Billy, he saw, was right next to him.

"Hey, how're you doing?" Billy said. "I was going

to call you and tell you I was coming to this thing, but I never got around to it."

"Me, too," said Doug.

"Ready?" Red called out from the front of the pack. "Let's go!"

"Catch you later," said Billy.

Doug nodded.

Off they went, following their leader. Red set a nice, easy pace. Neither Doug nor Billy had any problem keeping up with him. A few girls eager to show off pulled up almost alongside him, but he waved them back. Otherwise the ride was uneventful. Even on the way back when Red was observing them, they resisted the natural temptation to push a little harder. Everyone stayed at pretty much the same pace.

"Not bad," said Red back in the parking lot. "Let's all get together Monday afternoon at three for an indoor training session. From then on, we'll be pretty much outside. We'll have once a week, Saturday morning talks inside, but the real work is done on the road."

"So, how'd we do?" asked one of the girls, who Doug had discovered was named Jenny.

"Well, Jen, I'll tell you that none of you is ready for

76

the Tour de France, but I see some potential," said Red. "We'll let it go at that."

He went off to talk with a few club members.

"We'll leave in a few minutes, okay?" he called back to Doug. "Catch your breath. If you want, there's a machine inside that has chilled bottled water. Do you need any change?"

"Nope, I've got lots," said Doug.

When Red moved away, Doug looked around and saw that Billy was still there — and he was wiping off his forehead with his bandanna.

"Hey," Doug called over. "I'm going to get something cold to drink inside. Can I get you one?"

"Sure, that'd be great, said Billy. "I've got a pretty long trip back home, and the stuff in my bottle here is probably pretty warm by now."

When they were sipping their drinks, Doug asked Billy, "So what brought you here?"

"I was going to ask you the same thing," said Billy with a little laugh.

"Red told me about it," said Doug.

"Me, too," said Billy. "I guess you guys are pretty good pals."

Doug sipped his drink and told Billy how great it

was having Red staying at the carriage house. As they talked, he even confessed how worried he was about looking like a penguin at his sister's wedding when the time came.

"Hah!" Billy laughed. "And I probably look like a giraffe to some people! What a pair, huh?"

"Yeah, we're just a couple of animals," said Doug.

They clinked water bottles in a silent toast.

7

"Half day?"

Doug nodded.

Jimmy Bannister crushed the soda can with his right hand and tossed it into the rubbish bag. "Boy, some guys have it made," he said. But before Doug could start to explain, Jimmy went on, "Hey, just kidding. Red told me he's got big plans for you later on. He's taking off a little early, too. You go on and show 'em your stuff, kid." He turned and headed back to the work crew.

Red had suggested that Doug might want to take the afternoon off and work the next one instead. They'd agreed he'd work Mondays, Wednesdays, and Fridays on the Rails to Trails project. It was getting to the point where even Doug could see the progress they were making. The old railbed was slowly but surely being replaced by a recreation track.

He could even see a little progress of his own.

At first, he'd been the project's "gofer" — he'd "go fer" whatever anyone else needed — but now he was called to lend a hand on most of the strenuous jobs. The worst was a messy pile of old railroad ties. They'd obviously been there for years and were partially rotted. It had to be cleaned up right away for scheduled work to continue.

Tommy Lopardo had called over to Doug to give them a hand. Doug hefted a tie under each arm and lugged them away to the dump pile.

Andy Potts, thinking Doug was beyond hearing, had commented, "who would've thought that the fat kid who showed up here a couple of weeks ago would ever be able to do that?"

At first, that had made Doug angry. But he quickly realized that Andy hadn't meant to be cruel. The truth was, Doug *hadn't* been able to do the heavy work — not at the beginning of the summer, anyway. But since he'd started working on his cycling he felt better all around. Now he *could* give them a hand.

He put in his full effort that Monday morning and, following Red's advice, left at lunchtime.

When he got home, no one was there, so he checked the refrigerator. Lots of good things inside. He could make himself a hero sandwich with cheese and mayo and mustard, just the way he liked it. Then a big drink of milk, followed by a piece of leftover blueberry pie.

Instead, he made salad with lots of lettuce and thick slices of tomato. He added some sliced cold chicken and a splash of his mom's own salad dressing. She always kept a jar of it in the refrigerator.

As he dug in, he realized that Red's good eating habits just might be getting to him.

After cleaning up, he decided he deserved a little rest. It was off to the porch for a quick nap. Fifteen minutes later, a voice told him it was time to go over to the cycling club.

"Come on, Doug, time to get rolling," called Red from the driveway.

Doug leapt up. He felt rested and raring to go.

At the club, he discovered that the group had shrunk to nine. Two of the girls and one guy had dropped out. But he was pleased to see that Billy was there. They gave each other the thumbs-up sign.

Red gathered the group of six boys and three girls, with their bikes, into a circle.

"Okay," he said. "I'm going to go over some basic pointers and I'm going to use Doug here to demonstrate. I got Doug started out on his first twelve-speed racer a few weeks ago —"

Doug preened under Red's attention.

"But, believe me, he's as much a beginner as the rest of you."

That took a little of the stuffing out of Doug's chest.

Red then proceeded to work with each of them. He started with getting comfortable in the saddle.

"Put one foot on the pedal," he said. "Slip it into the toe clip. The tip of your other foot should just barely touch the ground. You'll be able to push off and then slip that second foot in. If you put both of them in and you're not leaning against something, you're going to keel over."

That makes sense, Doug realized. He'd just done it that way from the beginning without thinking about it. Red was great at making things come together in your head.

"Okay, what about your hands? What's the best place for them on the handlebars? Let's take a look," Red said. He showed them how different positions affected their riding comfort — and their ability to control the brakes.

"My own favorite is above the brake hoods," he said. "I just let my palms rest lightly on the hoods so that I can react quickly when I need to."

After a few more pointers on riding comfort and bike handling, he talked about safety.

"It's a good idea, too, for us to go over basic safety," he said. He read off a checklist that covered the basic traffic rules:

- *Always wear a helmet.*
- *Obey all traffic rules.*
- *Always ride on the right side of the road, in the same direction as the traffic.*
- *Wait your turn at intersections.*
- *Don't sneak up on cars stopped at traffic lights.*
- *Always turn from the proper lane — no shortcuts.*

- *Always give a hand signal before turning.*
- *Never weave in and out of traffic.*
- *Be extra careful passing parked cars.*
- *Watch out for pedestrians — you never know what they're going to do.*
- *Check your bike before setting off — especially the brakes.*

"Plus there're others for riding at night, but none of you should be doing that yet, so let's just say, 'Don't ride at night,' " Red concluded.

Doug, remembering his accident, could have added that you shouldn't go faster than you're able to see in front of you — but he figured that would sound stupid. Not everyone rode at breakneck speed when they didn't really know the road they were on.

"One final thing before we hit the road," said Red. "Right now, you should just be concentrating on learning how to get comfortable with your bikes. Nobody's interested in how fast you can go. This isn't a race. No one is going to come in first, second, third — or last. The idea is just to learn how to enjoy what you're doing, and to do it well. Got that?"

Everyone shouted out their agreement.

It was a good thing that Red's talk didn't last much longer. Doug could hardly wait to get out on the road and do his stuff. He was still a bit cocky about having a little jump on the rest of the group.

When they finally did take to the road, he found himself pushing just a little to stay close behind Red. Once in a while, one of the others overtook him. It took him completely by surprise when he discovered he really didn't like that.

But one of his most enjoyable times was when Billy rode up alongside him. They didn't talk while they were out on the road, but there was a definite communication between them. Doug noticed Billy glancing over, as if to take some tips. It made him feel good.

The route that Red had chosen was the same as on Saturday. It consisted mostly of straightaways and a few regular right-angle turns. There were no dangerous curves or tough hills to climb.

Since it was his second time on that same route, Doug could relax a little. He discovered that it felt good just to ride along. Now and then, Red would drop back or pull alongside one of the riders and call out some instruction.

"Head up and eyes on the road!"

"Steady pace, easy does it!"

"Where's that turn signal? Get that arm out!"

The only time he came up to Doug, he called over in a quiet voice, "Nice going," and moved right on ahead.

They were homeward bound when Doug noticed that Billy had pulled up a long way ahead of him. In fact, he was trailing Red so closely, you could almost call it tailgating. So far nobody had committed that mistake and Red hadn't commented on it.

But Doug knew, instinctively, that it wasn't a smart thing to do. He was too far back to call out to Billy and warn him. He had to get a little closer.

A bit of tension crept into Doug's body as he started to make his move. He tried to remember everything Red had taught him way back about shifting gears and changing his pace. But the gear thing was still tricky. He decided that he'd go the old-fashioned way and just pedal harder.

It was hard, slow work. But gradually, he got within hailing distance of Billy's back. He was about to call ahead when he realized the sound might not carry. After all, it seemed as though Red wasn't able to hear

Billy so close behind. His only choice was to come up alongside Billy.

Warning messages flashed inside his head. He could hear Red telling the group, "If you want to ride side by side, be sure there's room on the road, good visibility, and not much traffic."

Doug checked off the list. There was plenty of room since they were on a road with a wide, well-paved breakdown lane. Visibility was clear. His target was within his sight.

Traffic. That was the problem. There were lots of trucks out this afternoon that hadn't been there on Saturday. This time of day, a lot of people were heading home and the road was well traveled by all kinds and sizes of vehicles. Up until now, the group had kept single file to the far right-hand side of the breakdown lane. Even if a motor vehicle encroached on that area, there was a reasonable margin of safety.

Doug glanced over his shoulder to the left. The congested road had caused the motor vehicle traffic to slow down a little. Good, he thought, that'll keep 'em slow and steady.

He figured he'd have just the one shot, so he had to go all out. Reaching back into his memory, he shifted gears, silently praying he had done the right thing.

A change in the pressure and response to his pedaling told him something had happened. At the same time, he could see the distance between him and Billy getting smaller. It was working.

He pulled up to Billy's left side and called over, "Pull back! You're practically on top of him!"

It took a moment for his words to sink in. At first, Billy looked over at him as if he hadn't a clue. Then he got it. He slowed down the pace of his pedaling. The distance between him and Red gradually opened up.

At the same time, Doug let his own pace slacken. He was starting to drop back behind Billy when he suddenly heard a roaring sound to his rear.

It could only mean one thing: a vehicle coming up behind him.

Before he could even think of what to do, an open-top sports rec vehicle came gunning down the breakdown lane. It passed all the other bikers, then, without slowing for an instant, zoomed by Doug. It seemed to miss him by inches.

It also kicked up a lot of dust. Some found its way into Doug's nose and mouth and eyes. For a few seconds, he coughed and sputtered before gaining back his vision. By then he could see that he was almost back in line behind Billy where he belonged.

When they reached the clubhouse, Billy quickly dismounted and came running over to him.

"Boy, I'm really sorry for what happened out there," he said. "Are you okay?"

"Yeah, just a little grossed out from all the filth that got kicked up," said Doug, wiping his face with the bottom of his T-shirt. "How come you were following so close, anyhow? You know that can be dangerous. You don't have any room to maneuver if anything happens."

"You're right," said Billy. "I just forgot to pay attention. Before I knew it, there you were shouting at me. It threw me for a minute."

"But you got the message," said Doug.

"Sure, but I put you in danger," said Billy. "That really bums me out."

"Well, I'm okay," said Doug. "Hey, we'd better go inside and listen to what Red has to say."

As they took their seats, Red was just starting to outline a training program for those who were still interested in becoming what he called "competent" cyclists. It involved regular exercise and a daily practice routine. Records had to be kept and would be discussed at future group meetings. He then handed out copies of the training program.

Doug took one look and shook his head. At first, he couldn't see how he could do it all. He felt like a juggler trying to keep a whole lot of things up in the air at the same time. There was his new workout routine, cycling practice, the Rails to Trails project, helping out getting ready for the wedding — and there were only eight weeks left of summer vacation to do it all in! Maybe he could cut down on something.

Just as quickly, he realized he didn't want to cut down on anything. He liked what he was doing. He felt good. He wanted to keep feeling that way. Somehow or other, he'd find a way to work it out. Maybe he could talk it over with Red and put together a personal schedule.

Billy's eyes were as wide as saucers as he looked at the training program.

"Sure's going to take a lot of work," he said. "That's the part I don't really like much. But I guess we just have to do it!"

"You betcha," said Doug.

They looked up at each and burst out laughing.

8

"It says here that the video arcade was completely covered by insurance," said Mr. Cannon, looking up from the evening paper. It was two weeks after the Lakeridge Cycling Club's first ride together. He and Doug had gone out to the porch after dinner. As usual, Doug was stretched out on the swing.

"Are they going to rebuild?" he asked his father. "That'll take forever."

"Not right away," came the reply. "No, they're looking for some vacant space downtown to relocate. Hope to be open in a few weeks."

Doug brightened up. He was sore and achy from his cycling exertions. Maybe playing some videos would be just the kind of break from routine he needed.

Red had agreed that Doug could count his rides to and from the Rails project as part of his training program. When he sat down with Doug to go over the plan, Red had carefully worked out the time and effort it took to get to the job site by traveling different routes. He figured how much rest there ought to be after each trip, how much actual on-the-job stuff Doug did, and so on and so forth. Finally, he had a neat chart with everything on it for the five working days of the week.

"Weekends are completely up to you, pal," he said.

Doug's eyes grew huge. "Wow! This is a real serious, honest-to-goodness fitness program!"

Red laughed. "Of course it is! Fitness is nothing more than getting into shape. Only with this program, you're getting into shape *and* developing a special skill at the same time. Hey, it's two for the price of one!"

"Gee, thanks a lot," said Doug, looking a little bit skeptical.

"You just watch," said Red with a laugh. "You're gonna love it."

By this time, Doug had survived the purchase of some decent cycling clothes. Mrs. Cannon had volunteered to take him over to the mall to pick them out. But Doug had a different plan in mind. He arranged to meet Mr. Cannon at his office one lunch hour. Together, they visited a specialty sporting goods store some distance from the mall.

Mr. Cannon waited quietly while Doug tried on different outfits and finally selected a shirt and shorts combo that didn't make him look too much like a blimp. Still, he vowed to wear the outfit only when biking. With the helmet and goggles he already had, he figured he'd look okay.

At first, Doug thought his father didn't approve of what he had picked out. But then Mr. Cannon had pulled out his charge card and asked the sales clerk to bring three more of each item to the counter. As they were being rung in, Doug thanked his father.

"I consider it money well spent, son," he replied.

Suited up in his new gear, Doug had faced his first week of real training with enthusiasm. In fact, the only thing bothering him had nothing to do with biking. As the summer days ticked along, it was the wedding — and the tuxedo and the as-yet-unbought wedding gift — that weighed on his mind.

Now, sitting on the front porch, Mr. Cannon inadvertently gave Doug an idea about how to solve one of those two problems.

"Oh, by the way, I saw something in the paper that

might interest you," said Mr. Cannon. "There was a small item that said Jack Millman, the head of the Lakeridge Cycling Club, just announced that they're going to hold a charity event. Called it the Tour de Lakeridge. Sounds pretty fancy, but it said it's for all ages and levels. You know anything about that?"

Doug scratched his head.

"Oh, yeah, he mentioned that the first day I went over to the club. But I don't really know much about it. I'll check with Red."

On Monday, when they took their midday break at the Rails to Trails project, Doug asked Red about this Tour de Lakeridge. As soon as he mentioned the subject, Red was all smiles.

"Darn! Newspaper beat me to it!" he said. Then he showed Doug a roll of posters he'd brought along in his backpack that day. They were greenish blue, with a picture of a racing cyclist and all the words in white.

"I could use some help putting them up around town," said Red.

They look real neat, Doug thought. "Sure," he said. "But what *is* it, anyhow? Sounds French."

Red explained that a "tour de" was just a cycling term for a "trip around" somewhere. And this particular tour was a charity event. It was also an unofficial tour. The results didn't go into any record book.

In this case, there were a number of different routes of different lengths so that anybody could enter. The idea was for participants to get people to pledge a certain amount of money per mile. Then the bikers would complete the circuit and collect the donations. The proceeds all went to charity.

"The club has participated in a number of these events, but this is the first time we've had one of our own,"said Red.

"How come?" asked Doug.

"It's a lot of work getting it organized," Red replied, thumping the posters. "Plus you really need a good-size membership to start off with. Of course, anyone can enter, not just members. So it could be pretty big."

"Sounds like it's way out of my league,"said Doug.

"Nope," said Red.

"What? Did I hear you right? Are you saying I could take part in a real race?" Doug asked.

"It's not a race," said Red. "It's a *challenge*. You're setting a goal for yourself and trying to reach it — along with a pack of other riders."

"Hmmmmmm," said Doug. "Well, I'll help you put up the posters, but I don't know about doing anything else."

"Fine," said Red. "But in case you do get interested, here's a little brochure that tells you the rules. It has an application inside, too. By the way, how many miles are you doing a day now?"

"Let me see," said Doug. "On days I work, back and forth to the project is about six. And I do five miles on my own later. Eleven. I ride about a little more or less on other days."

"The basic ride in the Tour is only twelve miles. And the event is still two weeks off," said Red. A shout came from behind them. "Hey, we'd better give those guys a hand filling in that hole over there."

He leapt to his feet and headed off toward the work crew.

Doug stared at the cover of the brochure, then tucked it in his pocket. He followed Red slowly, his mind filled with a whole range of new thoughts: Was this something he could do? And was it something he wanted to do?

He decided he'd have to give it a lot more thought. That day, on the way back home, he had a hard time staying behind Red. He found himself pushing just a little harder.

When he arrived home, he parked his bike and went in the back door. On the kitchen table was a note from his mother. She and Kate were down at the mall doing something about bridesmaid's dresses. Dinner might be a little late. There was a batch of newly baked brownies on the counter.

Doug looked at the brownies, but what he really wanted was a tall drink of water. He chugged it down and left the kitchen to go change his clothes. The brownies could wait.

Up in his room, he took out the brochure and read it carefully.

- *To benefit a group of local charities.*
- *A pleasant, scenic 12-mile loop.*
- *Rest stops are provided along each course.*
- *Will be held rain or shine.*
- *Each entrant will receive a specially designed Tour de Lakeridge T-shirt.*
- *The top three finishers in each level will receive a Tour de Lakeridge commemorative water bottle. The*

*first-place winner will also receive a
silver trophy bowl.*
- *There will be a post-tour picnic in the
park opposite the clubhouse.*
- *The registration fee is one dollar for
each mile of your event — or five
times that number in collected
pledges. Donations can be made in
your own name or as a tribute to
someone of your choice.*

Phew! That told him a lot. And through it all, one
thought wouldn't go away: How could he face Red if
he didn't take part? Wasn't this the sort of thing even
beginner cyclists had to do? What's that thing his
mom called it whenever he did something big — a
rite of passage?

It looked like this passage was going to be a twelve-
mile ride. For an instant, an image from a faraway
dream passed through his head. "Can-non! Cannon!" screamed a crowd of fans. Doug looked down
at the pamphlet in his hands.

It may be a far cry from the Olympics, he thought.
But it's a step.

He wondered whether Billy Torrant would enter the race. It would be kind of fun to have a buddy out there. Then he thought of someone else he'd like to have out there. Someone who loved cycling. An idea took root in his head.

That evening, he took his father aside.

"Dad, are you going to be in your office tomorrow?" he asked.

"Sure," said Mr.Cannon. "Why?"

"Mind if I stop by?"

"Of course you can," said Mr. Cannon. "Anytime you like."

The next day was an off day for the Rails to Trails project. Doug did his practice run, then got cleaned up and went down to Mr. Cannon's office. He was armed with a pledge book he had picked up from Red earlier.

"Dad," he said. "Will you sign up to sponsor me for the Tour de Lakeridge? See, it's a charity event. You pledge to pay so much if I complete the distance I sign up for."

"Doug, nothing would make me happier than to be a sponsor. Where do I sign?" asked his father.

He took the pen, started to sign, then stopped.

99

"What's this?" he asked, pointing to a notation Doug had added to the pledge form.

"The money collected is being donated to cancer research. Riders can leave that space blank and donate their collections anonymously. Or they can write in someone's name and give the money on behalf of that person. I decided to fill it in. But don't tell, okay? I want it to be a surprise."

Mr. Cannon grinned, signed, and handed the book back to Doug.

"Is it okay if I ask a few of the others?"

"Go right ahead," said Mr. Cannon. "They hit me up often enough, and this is definitely a worthwhile cause."

Doug circled the office and collected quite a few sponsors with generous pledges. He thanked everyone and was heading out the door when he heard his father's longtime assistant, Mr. Atwood, say quietly, "I can hardly believe that's Doug Cannon. He's really trimmed down and looks so healthy!"

Doug couldn't see it, but someone else had overheard the same remark. Inside his office, Mr. Cannon's chest swelled with pride.

9

Collecting pledges turned out to be the easy part. Getting himself prepped was a lot harder.

It wasn't simply practicing the twelve-mile run. He knew he could do that. It was everything else — like showing himself cycling in front of a zillion people. Despite the nice comments he heard, like the one in his father's office, there were still a few people who still saw the old Doug Cannon when they looked at him.

He tried to avoid checking himself out in the mirror, but he still caught glimpse of bulges here and there. Those rolls didn't just disappear like magic. He still had a way to go.

And what if something unexpected happened during the event. Pepper Meade and the gang were due back any day. Leave it to them to do something stupid like throw banana peels in front of him. That's just the sort of thing they'd think was funny. Well, maybe they wouldn't even know the event was taking place — much less that he was in it.

Doug groaned. There were so many things that could go wrong. Maybe he ought to just chuck it all and spend his time practicing video games on his computer. Someday the arcade would reopen.

His thoughts were interrupted by Kate shouting to his mother in the dining room. "I'll be there in a minute," she said. "I want to watch the local news on TV to see the long-range weather forecast."

"Well, I'm ready for dinner," said Doug. "I'm starved."

They were camped on the living room floor watching TV.

As he got up to leave, the TV announcer caught him by surprise.

"A final note before the weather. The video arcade damaged by fire will be open for business at its new location in just a week. The grand opening is scheduled for next Saturday."

Next Saturday! The same day as the Tour de Lakeridge! Rats! Well, it would just have to wait.

Doug had been training hard for the past week. He'd collected a slew of pledges and had turned in his registration form.

He'd also studied the course. He found out exactly where the rest stops would be and worked that into his training schedule. It was good to know that he wouldn't have to go the full twelve miles without a stop.

Most of the kids in his beginners' group in the club had also entered the event, including Billy. One had to go off to the seashore with her family, so she couldn't. Another one just didn't feel up to it.

During the past Saturday training session, Red had gone over everything he thought they should know. His closing advice was, "Remember, this isn't an official competition. You'll probably have a lot more events like this in your lives. But it's your first, so try to enjoy it. And good luck."

By that point, Doug knew for sure that he could do the course. The question was, would he disgrace himself by coming in last? He knew it wasn't a race, but he didn't want to be the last one in his group to cross the line. And again, the chance of a surprise, what if he didn't finish at all? How could he show up at the picnic after that?

The picnic, that was something else to think about. There'd probably be lots of people he knew there. Maybe he could simply do the course, then slip away without going to the picnic. Instead,he could zip over to the arcade and try out any new machines they had.

Kate clicked off the TV and said, "No big weather news. Let's eat. Hey, you need to make sure you're getting all your vitamins. You'll need all your strength for Saturday. That reminds me, we have to talk strategy. Oh, I know, Red's a good coach, but I am what's called a veteran observer. I can give you a pointer or two."

"Are you planning to watch it? I mean, are you really interested in it?" Doug asked.

"Are you kidding? Terry and I are going to watch it from the start. Then we're going to cut across so we can see you go by about midway. And then we're going to zip over to see you come in at the finish," she said. "Mom and Dad will meet us there with some extra treats for the picnic."

"Great," said Doug, sitting down at the table.

That takes care of any plans to hit the arcade. I'll have to wait until Monday, he decided.

The scene in front of the Lakeridge Cycling Club on Saturday was something Doug could never have imagined. There were hundreds of cyclists all decked out in full gear. They were walking, leaning on, straddling, or simply holding on to a huge variety of bikes. Half the people had white cards with jet-black numbers on the front and back of their shirts. Others were standing in line waiting for theirs to be handed out.

Edging his way through the crowd, Doug found the registration desk with "A to F" posted on a sign above it.

"Cannon, Douglas Cannon," he said to the gray-haired man seated in front of a large file box.

"Right, here you are. Number 603. I hope it's a lucky one for you," came the reply. "Oh, you're in the twelve-mile course. It doesn't begin for another two hours. That is the right one, isn't it?"

"Uh-huh," said Doug. "I just wanted to be here for the very beginning. I don't want to miss any part of it."

A few minutes later, the gun went off as the fiftymilers took off on their long, grueling ride. An hour later the thirty-milers would take to the road.

"Gosh, I don't know how they do it!"

"Has anyone seen my kid sister?"

"Don't forget, we'll meet at the picnic."

"Where'd I leave my bike?"

"Twelve miles and it's mostly uphill!"

The noise built steadily as the crowd grew and grew. Doug was bounced back and forth until he knew he had to get out of the way for a minute. He didn't think he was nervous, but suddenly he couldn't sit still.

He wandered into the club to fill his water bottle with fresh, cold water. Maybe that would cool him off a little. He just had to stay calm and focused. After all, it was just a simple twelve-mile ride. Piece of cake. Sure!

He was screwing on the cap when a familiar form sporting number 636 appeared in front of him.

"Hey, you're early, too," he said to Billy Torrant.

"Yeah," said Billy, walking by him.

Doug was startled. That's it? he thought. Nothing else to say, like "Good luck" or "May the best man win" or anything like that? Then he considered. Hey,

106

maybe he's just concentrating — and that's exactly what I should do, too.

He wandered outside, where he found himself a quiet, shady patch of grass under a tree. It was a great place to do his warm-up exercises. He hated them, but he knew how important they were.

When the twelve-milers finally lined up for their start, there were a lot of unfamiliar faces. Some were kids his age. Some were a little bit older. And some were real veterans, with lots of gray hair showing from under their helmets. In fact, in all this crowd, Doug was hard pressed to pick out the handful from his training group who had actually shown up. Except for Billy, of course. Even if his number 636 wasn't visible, his height always made him a standout.

As he waited for the starting gun, Doug wiggled his fingers to loosen the tension. He could feel his pulse throbbing in his wrists and at the side of his forehead. It seemed to climb higher and higher as the wait stretched out. Deep breaths, he told himself. Long, deep breaths.

A zillion thoughts came rushing into his head like a flood. Was he going to make a fool of himself? Did he look silly in his racing gear? Did it really matter whether he did well or not?

Bang!

The race was on. No more time for wasteful thoughts. Every effort had to be concentrated on his cycling. It was the one thing that had to be in the forefront of his mind at all times.

He started out pedaling like a madman, possessed with one desire: to zoom straight out there. Even though Red had gone over strategy with him, he forgot everything about keeping up a steady pace.

Then he saw her: Kate. She was waving at him. No, she was pushing her arms down and shouting something. Peace! No, *pace,* that was it. She was telling him to slow down and keep a steady pace.

He got the message. He started pedaling a nice, smooth, regular stroke. He put the stress on the back as he rode through the upstroke, solid and regular. It put him smack in the center of the pack as they rode along a level stretch. For the first mile or so, there was some dropping back and pulling forward by the other cyclists. Without glancing to one side or another, he could see a couple of familiar riders dropping out of the main pack to the rear. Neither of them was wear-

ing number 636. Billy was nowhere in sight at the moment.

The course changed to a gradual uphill climb as it approached the first of two rest stops. Doug shifted gears to let the bike do some of the work. He was tempted to rise up from the saddle like he used to do on his old bike, but Red had taught him that you get more power by sliding back on the saddle. He also adjusted his pedaling speed to the new challenge.

All of that training worked. The first four miles sped by cleanly. When he arrived at the rest stop, he felt a lot better than he ever thought he would. He called out his number to one of the timekeepers, who scribbled it down on his recording chart. A quick glance at the time clock told him that he was right on the target he'd set with Red. They'd based it on Doug's experience, the average for similar races they'd looked up, and the goal they thought best for him. Since the winners would be determined by the best time, he had to pay attention to the clock.

He also saw that Billy had pulled in only seconds after him. The two beginners were making a pretty good show of it so far. But Billy still didn't seem to want to talk when Doug caught his eye.

If that's the way he wants to be, okay, thought Doug. But I hope it's not because I'm a little bit ahead. I'm not really out to beat him.

Or am I? How would I feel if he was ahead of me?

Hmmm . . . I'm just glad he isn't.

Rested, Doug called out his number again and sped off as the timekeeper jotted it down.

The next leg of the tour was a lot more challenging than the first part. The terrain had changed and there were a number of sharp turns to deal with. Doug knew that it was too early for him to make any kind of a break for the front of the pack, but he certainly didn't want to drop behind, either. Instead, he practiced another tip that Red had passed on to the training group. To keep up his speed on a sharp turn, he pedaled harder and entered it faster. That way he didn't have to pedal through the curve. The momentum took him through it.

By the second rest stop, he figured that he was one of about six at the head of the pack as he listened to the times being announced by the checkers. He wasn't sure of how it had happened, but he was very proud of himself. He only wished he could see Kate or Terry or his folks. He knew that Red was stuck down at the finish line as one of the official recorders. Those were the people he cared most about right now. So what if his new friend Billy had turned out to be not so friendly.

In fact, for the moment, number 636 was nowhere in sight as the third and final stage began. There was so much talk at the pit stop, Doug knew that he was now pretty much neck and neck with just a few others — including Billy. Their times were that close. So it looked like it probably would be a real race down to the wire.

Doug got ready for the long, final push. He wasn't tired yet, but he could tell that his legs were tighter now than at the start. He jogged in place for a second to loosen them up before mounting his bike.

At first, the final stage didn't seem tough. But it quickly changed into a steep, roughly paved, downhill slope. Doug remembered from his test runs that this was where he had to keep his wits about him. To open up at breakneck speed to better his time was really tempting. But keeping control of his bike would be difficult under those circumstances. He had to find a happy medium.

In practice, this wasn't all that hard to do — with

112

no one around. But now, he could almost feel the heavy breathing behind him.

Some of the other riders obviously didn't feel the same way. A few of them went sailing by him as he held to his own speed.

"Caution!" Red's word stuck out in his mind. Don't give in to temptation. In the long run, a steady, controlled pace will pay off.

No sooner had these words come into his mind, when Billy came from out of nowhere and passed him on a long, straight portion.

Well, let him. I'll stick to what I've learned, thought Doug as the straightaway turned into a curve to the left.

Doug slowly applied his brakes to ease the pressure as he banked to make the curve. Two riders in front of him didn't. They were going so fast, the sudden change got them and they went sailing off the road into an open field before losing balance and falling.

Billy wasn't one of them. He had managed to survive the wicked downhill turn in his own way.

Now it was definitely time to put on all the pressure as they hit the last mile or so.

Doug used every ounce of energy and brainpower

to stay out in front with a few others. As far as he could tell, he was trailing only three other riders as they came closer and closer to the finish line. Number 636 was right in front of him.

The kids in Doug's group weren't ready for tricky maneuvers yet, Red had said. At this stage in their cycling experience, they would be wiser to keep away from others and just ride their own race. So creeping up on Billy and crowding him out wouldn't be the smartest thing to do — even though it sure looked possible. Instead, Doug gave him a wide berth as he pumped his legs for all he was worth.

He could feel his heart pounding. The sweat was pouring down his face and his shirt was sticking to his back. He couldn't remember when he'd ever felt so hot and feverish — and wasn't lying in a sickbed with something like the measles!

But he also knew he couldn't stop. *Wouldn't* stop. He had to keep pressing. He needed to gain those few precious seconds that could make all the difference in the end.

Inch by inch, then foot by foot, and then — *whoosh* — he passed Billy wide on his right side.

Off in the distance, he could see the big sign with

the word FINISH stretched across the road. There were only two riders in front of him.

But Billy was only a few feet behind. Doug had to keep up the pace to come in in the top three — making him a real winner in everyone's eyes. He just couldn't let Billy beat him out altogether.

There was a tremendous roar in his ears as the sound of the crowd thundered all about him. It surrounded him like a mysterious force that helped to push him forward.

He could hear his own breath gasping in his ears. Still, he strained on to stay in front.

Then, suddenly, something happened. The rider in front of him froze. His stroke became wobbly and he just managed to pull over to the side of the road. There was a look of agony as he clutched his calf and rolled on the ground.

Muscle cramp! It had to be!

The shock broke Doug's stride. Concern for the rider who had gotten so close had taken his mind off his own ride for a split second.

It was just enough to give Billy that edge he needed. Doug caught his eye as he came up abreast and inched slightly forward.

The two riders passed the finish line neck and neck in what had to be a photo finish. Except that there was no official camera. The actual winner was determined by the timekeeper. The top three spots would be awarded strictly according to their records.

No matter what, Doug figured he probably had achieved his goal of not making a complete fool of himself. And he knew he would have had a shot at a top spot even if nothing had happened to the rider in front of him. He hadn't needed a stroke of luck to make it.

He dismounted and began his cool-down exercises on the spot. All he wanted was to soak his entire body in an icy tub, but he knew that wasn't going to happen. He gradually unwound the way he had learned was best.

The next thing he knew, though, he was surrounded by Kate, Terry, his mom and dad — and Red. The latter had taken a break from his job as a record keeper.

"Fantastic work!" said Red, beaming with pleasure.

"I am so proud of you," Kate said. "And I don't care

how sweaty you are, I have to give you this hug." She wrapped her arms around him and pressed her cheek against his.

His dad and mom hugged him, too. Terry then said, "Yuck, how's about this instead?" then offered him ten. Doug's hands were still so wet, he practically slid off the slap and return.

When he finally had his breath back, Doug had one question.

"What were the final results?"

Red delivered the answer.

"The judges gave second place to Billy. You came in third by a fraction of a second."

For a moment, Doug's heart sank a tiny bit. He finished behind Billy! Hey, wait a minute, that's not what this was about! He bounced back the very next second when Red went on, "But as far as I'm concerned, you rode a great ride — and in my book, you're number one."

And his ear-to-ear grin proved he meant every word.

10

A little while later, the Cannon family and friends had settled down around their red-checkered cloth to enjoy the post-tour celebration. Mrs. Cannon opened up her picnic cooler chest and took out a plate of deviled eggs.

"Mom! You're the greatest! I could eat the whole plate of 'em!" said Doug. But at the very moment he was saying those words, he knew that he couldn't. Before he had started cycling, it would have been a different story. Now he knew that his stomach had shrunk at least a little bit. There just didn't seem to be the same room inside.

"Thanks for the compliment, but I think we ought to pass them around," said Mrs. Cannon.

Doug smiled and took one egg off the plate. He let

it sit on the small dish in front of him instead of wolfing it down in one gulp, the way he used to.

"I hope we have these at the wedding," Terry said. "I love 'em, too."

That started a round of wedding talk. When would the bridesmaids' dresses be delivered? Had Kate and Terry picked out their rings yet? How many tiers should the wedding cake be? And, then, the questions that sent shivers up Doug's spine: What about the ushers? When will they be fitted for their tuxedos?

"I think I'll go change out of these riding clothes," said Doug. "I'll be back in a minute."

He started to get up, when a voice coming through a megaphone stopped him.

"Your attention, please! It is now time to award the prizes to today's winners. If our top three riders in each distance would please join me up on the stage," Jack Millman announced.

With an embarrassed but happy grin, Doug headed toward the stage. His family followed at his heels. A moment later, he was standing next to Billy and the first-place winner of the twelve-mile race.

When his name was called, he stepped forward and accepted his commemorative water bottle amid the cheers of the crowd.

Jack Millman had one final thing to say. "We've raised a good amount of money toward cancer research. But the person who raised the single greatest amount of pledges deserves a round of applause." Jack checked his sheet, frowned, then quickly smiled. "Well, it seems someone is about to get a nice surprise. Kate Cannon, will you please join us up here?"

Doug couldn't stop smiling as his startled sister climbed the steps to the stage. Jack motioned to him.

"A big round of applause for the fellow who collected the most pledges, Doug Cannon! And," he added before the clapping began, "another round for the person in whose name he collected that money, his sister, Kate!"

The crowd roared its approval. Kate blushed, then grabbed Doug in a big hug.

"I wanted to give you something special for your wedding present," Doug whispered in her ear. "Hope you like it!"

The tears he saw in her eyes were the only answer he needed.

Before he went to bed that night, Doug soaked his body in a hot bath. Red had told him that he wouldn't have too many aches and pains after the race because he'd trained so hard. Doug wasn't so sure. The hot bath definitely felt good. And when he collapsed into bed, he fell asleep in an instant.

It had been decided beforehand that he wouldn't work on the Rails to Trails project on the Monday after the bike race. Instead, he slept late and wandered down to the kitchen long after everyone else had finished breakfast. He had something on his mind and he decided today was the day to confront it.

Mrs. Cannon came in off the porch when she heard him.

"Today is your day of rest, Douglas," she said. "I'll fix you a nice breakfast. How about pancakes?"

"Um, I'll just have my usual," he replied.

"Just orange juice and cold cereal? Doesn't sound too exciting," she said. "Are you sure?"

"Uh-huh," he said. "Maybe I'll have some strawberries on top of the cereal."

"Might as well," said Mrs. Cannon. "You skipped the strawberry shortcake yesterday."

"I'm just not all that hungry these days," said Doug.

"Well, maybe now that your favorite haunt is back in business that'll change," said Mrs. Cannon. "You always came back from the video arcade with a big appetite." She added some sliced strawberries to Doug's bowl of cereal. "Or is something else on your mind?"

"No, it's nothing . . . I mean . . . well, it isn't that big a deal, but . . . I don't know," he stammered.

"All right, Douglas, what have you done? Have you broken something?"

"No! It's nothing like that!" Doug said. "It's . . . it's about the wedding."

"What about the wedding?" asked Mrs. Cannon.

"It's about being an usher and having to wear one of those stupid-looking penguin suits!" he almost shouted.

"Calm down," said Mrs. Cannon. "Your reaction is perfectly normal. I've never heard of any man or boy who didn't hate the idea of a tuxedo the first time he had to wear one. Once you have it on and see how nice you look, you'll get over it."

"I'll look like a dumb overstuffed — "

"Douglas! I won't have you saying that about yourself," said Mrs. Cannon. "You look wonderful. I haven't mentioned it, but you've really changed a lot this summer. That trail job has been so good for you. And cycling on top of it, well, it's like you're a new person. Not that the old one wasn't just fine. And, haven't you been complaining that your jeans have gotten too big — even for that ugly baggy look you love so much?"

He had to laugh. Mrs. Cannon thought that just about everything cool he wore was ugly. But she suffered silently. He could tell from the way her eyebrows shot up whenever he appeared in one of his new sloppy getups. Parents just didn't understand.

And no one would understand why he just didn't want to squeeze into any dumb tuxedo.

"Okay, okay," he said and started to wolf down his cereal.

Later that morning, Doug hopped on his bike and rode down to the newly opened video arcade. He had just finished checking out the layout when he heard a familiar voice.

"Yo, Doug, how's it going?"

It was Pepper Meade.

"Hey, you guys are back from hockey camp, huh?" Doug asked. "How was it?"

"Pretty good," said Pepper. "Saw you in the race the other day."

"Oh, yeah?"

"Yeah." Pepper continued to stare at him, but he didn't say anything more.

Doug found himself starting to redden.

"Yeah, well, I've been working out and . . . and stuff, you know," he stammered.

"Working out. Right. You must be down to just about a ton and a half now!" said Pepper. He burst into laughter at his own joke.

Doug made a half-hearted attempt to join him.

"Listen, me and the guys are going over to the ball-field for a pickup game of soccer later," said Pepper. "You wanna play?"

"Nah, I think I'd better get back home," said Doug. "My mom's got a list of things for me to do. My sister's getting married pretty soon. Lots to do."

"Married? That's cool," said Pepper. He followed Doug outside the arcade.

"See you," said Doug as he unlocked his bike and drew it out of the rack. He could feel Pepper's eyes on him.

"New bike?" asked Pepper. "That's the hottest thing on wheels any of the guys have. What're you doing with such a hot bike?"

"Like I said, I've been working out," said Doug. He put on his helmet and slipped his feet into the toe clips.

"Cycling, you mean?" Pepper called out as Doug took off.

But Doug simply waved back and said, "See you!"

A ton and a half! The words burned into his mind. Would the guys always think of him as just another lard bottom? He found he wasn't as good-natured about the kidding as he used to be. Next time, he thought he might give Pepper Meade something to think about.

He rode around aimlessly. There was no list at home waiting for him. He didn't want to see the guys on the trails project. He just needed a place to chill out for a while.

Then he realized he was only a few blocks away

from the clubhouse. Maybe there was something over there he could read or do for a little while till he calmed down.

As he pulled up in front of the clubhouse, he noticed that there were no bikes parked outside. On the front door there was a notice that said *"Closed on Mondays."*

The day was starting to warm up. Doug took off his helmet and wiped his brow. What was he going to do? Where was he going to go?

Since the guys were at the soccer field, maybe he ought to go to the beach. Nah, there'd be people he knew there, too. He didn't want to see any of his old friends right now.

But what about a new friend? Or at least someone he'd thought of as one?

After the race, Doug had wanted to talk things over with Billy. He still couldn't understand why Billy had given him the cold shoulder before the race and during the rest stops. Even on the platform, Billy had acted strange. Maybe it was just nerves, Doug thought. Anyhow, he wanted to congratulate his friend on coming in as one of the top three. But right after the awards were handed out, Billy had rushed off with some folks, probably his family. They hadn't even stayed for the picnic.

Doug remembered where Billy lived from his very first training session with Red — Cosgrove Street. It was a good ride from the clubhouse. Heck, it was worth a shot. If Billy was there, great. If he wasn't, well, it was still a good ride.

With his helmet back on, Doug started pedaling in the direction of Billy's house. Twenty minutes later, he rounded the corner of Cosgrove Street.

Doug pedaled down the street and pulled up in front of the Torrant house.

He was wondering whether it was such a good idea to barge in on Billy, when he saw his bike parked in the driveway. The house looked really nice. There were bright red and yellow flowers in the window boxes and a low, neatly clipped hedge.

Just then, Billy came out the side door and headed for his bike.

"Hey! Billy!" he called and rode up the drive-way.

Billy's look of surprise quickly turned into one of

pleasure. He greeted Doug with a big smile, then threw out his hand for a high five.

It was Doug's turn to be surprised — but he held his tongue.

"So what brings you over to Cosgrove Street?" Billy asked.

"Wise guy," said Doug. "I came by to see you, you know, to talk about the race and everything."

"Sure, great," said Billy. "Hey, you want something cold to drink?"

"Just water," said Doug.

"Come on around back," said Billy.

Doug followed him to a shaded patio behind the house. Billy went inside. He came back out a few minutes later with the woman Doug had seen after the race. "Doug, this is my mom," he said.

Doug got up and said, "Hi." He wondered whether she thought he was kind of heavy, especially next to her slender son.

"Nice to meet you, Doug," she said. "Billy said you just wanted water, but I've made some fresh fruit punch and thought you might like that."

She put down a pitcher and two glasses and then left the boys to themselves.

As they sipped their drinks in the cool, shady backyard, Doug relaxed. He decided to come right out and ask Billy about his behavior at the race.

Before he had half-finished his question, Billy interrupted him.

"I know, and I'm sorry," he explained. "You see, I get really uptight sometimes. I guess it's from having kids call me 'Stringbean' and things like that. So before the race, I just shut my mind to everything. All I could think about was what I had to do to get it over with."

"And afterward?" Doug asked.

"My stomach was still tied up in knots. I couldn't eat anything. I almost lost it up on the stage!"

Doug couldn't imagine that there was room in Billy's stomach for a knot, but he understood about feeling nervous and tense. So he simply said, "Well, I thought you rode a great race. Yeah, I know we're not supposed to think of it as a real race, but there were three winners, weren't there?"

"Uh-huh," said Billy. "And we were two of them." He raised his glass of punch and the two boys drank a toast.

It was at that moment that Doug realized how much

fun he had hanging out with Billy. Where Pepper Meade seemed to want to use him as a punching bag, someone to make fun of and to be the butt of his jokes, Billy took Doug seriously. Before, Doug had been willing to put up with Pepper. But this summer had shown him that he deserved better. Billy — and Red, too — had helped him see what real, honest friendship was.

Doug settled back more comfortably in his chair. With his new friends, his biking regimen, the Rails to Trails project, and his sister's wedding, he figured the weeks ahead were going to pass by swiftly.

11

But all that changed the next week.

It was the second Monday in August. Doug jumped out of bed, grabbed the first T-shirt he found in his drawer, and slipped it on without looking at it. When he saw what he was wearing, he blinked.

Hanging loosely on his frame was an orange T-shirt with green letters spelling out the words *"Rails to Trails."* It was the same shirt he had barely been able to squeeze into at the start of the summer.

"Might have to trade that in for a size medium," Red joked when Doug rode up beside him on the way to the project. "The way that's flapping in the breeze, you're creating too much wind resistance!"

"Guess I'll just have to slip behind you and draft for a while," Doug said as he did just that. "You don't mind pulling for me, do you?"

Red laughed. "Oh, no, not at all!" With a sly grin, he increased his speed and broke away, leaving Doug in the dust. Doug gave chase. He had almost caught him when they reached the site. He hopped off his bike and trotted over to where Red stood. Billy pulled in a moment later.

"You could at least *pretend* to be winded!" Billy said. With a start, Doug realized Billy was right — he wasn't gasping for breath even after the impromptu race. Red smiled knowingly, then turned away.

Well, what do you know about that? Doug thought as he rolled his bike to its usual resting spot near a big tree. Leaning it carefully against the trunk, he remembered his first day on the job. He had fallen asleep under this very tree and had a wonderful dream. An Olympic dream. Then, that dream had seemed unreal, impossible. But now . . .

Doug could hardly believe he was the same person who had had to dust off his old three-speed at the beginning of the summer.

Others felt the same way. He was no longer just a "gofer" on the Rails project. He readily lent a hand with some of the tougher jobs and was praised by his

coworkers for his willingness to do the dirty work. When he looked at the newly cleared sections of the path, Doug couldn't help feeling good about all he had helped to accomplish.

Doug's thoughts were interrupted by a call from the work crew leader. It was time for another morning of work. For Doug, it had become a labor of love. He knew how proud he was going to be the first time he used the bike trail he had helped create.

Jimmy Bannister, the project's leader, chased that happy future event away in the next moment.

"Well, I was hoping I wouldn't have to give this speech, but I don't see any way around it," Jimmy said. "Folks, we're just about out of money for this project. You can probably tell by looking around you that our volunteer numbers have dropped since the beginning of summer,too. There are five miles of trail left to clear and pave but no one to help do it. It was my hope that we'd be using this path by Labor Day weekend. But that's not going to happen. Not this Labor Day, anyhow."

Everyone was silent. They had all worked hard over the past weeks. To Doug, the news was like a punch in the stomach.

Red spoke up. "So we'll just find new sources of manpower and knock on the local shopkeepers' doors for donations a second time. We did it before, we can do it again!"

Doug looked at Jimmy hopefully. But Jimmy shook his head. "If there was just one mile of trail left, I'd say let's go for it. But it'd take at least two weeks to collect enough money and gather the people. By that time, everybody will be thinking ahead to school. Shopkeepers won't want to donate to an end-of-the-summer project. They'll want to spend their money sponsoring school teams, or some holiday event scheduled to take place in a few months, not in a year or so. Parents and students will be busy with school, with fall and winter projects, so they won't have time to help out. No, I'm afraid that in a week, we'll have to wrap things up here. At least until next summer."

Jimmy turned away sadly, leaving a stunned and disappointed crew behind him.

That afternoon, Doug and Billy rode off together. They had established a daily routine where they worked out on the Rails project in the mornings, ate a quick lunch, then biked on a carefully mapped-out route on the side streets. Every day they did at least twenty miles. Doug was seeing parts of Lakeridge he'd never known existed; and he had never felt or slept better in his life.

It had been such a lackluster day's labor on the bike path that for the first time all summer, they were happy to get away from it.

"Boy, I sure wish I had a million bucks to donate," Billy said.

"Yeah. I hate thinking that all our hard work was for nothing!" Doug replied. They pedaled along quietly for a while. Toward the end of their usual loop, they put on steam and rounded the corner of Doug's street at full speed. When they reached the driveway, they coasted to a stop and dismounted, huffing but feeling better for the exertion.

"Hey, isn't that Red?" Billy asked, pointing toward the carriage house.

"Yeah. Let's go say hi."

Red was sitting in the driveway, surrounded by bike parts.

"Why'd you take your bike apart?" Billy asked with curiosity.

"Cleaning it," was Red's reply. He finished greasing the part he was holding, then looked up at the boys. A wide grin spread across his face. "Got some news for you."

Doug's heart soared. Maybe the bike path project had been given new life.

"The Lakeridge Cycling Club is planning a trip to the Westwood Velodrome on Saturday. They're holding pre-Olympic trials!"

"Oh," Doug replied, disappointed. Then Red's words sank in. "Wait, did you say Olympic trials? Are you going?"

"Yep," Red replied. "And so are you and Billy."

Doug blinked. "We are?"

"Your folks all agreed that if you two wanted to, you could come with me. We'll be traveling by bus really early Saturday morning. We can be in the stands by ten o'clock, watching the indoor races."

"Indoor races?" Billy asked. "What're they like?"

"You'll see this weekend. Are you game?"

Doug and Billy were.

"I've heard that track races are a whole different

world from racing outdoors," Doug said. "I can't wait to check it out!"

"Me, either," Billy agreed.

When Saturday morning arrived, Doug, Red, and Billy were all in need of some cheering up. The Rails project had officially closed down the afternoon before and each of them was feeling a sense of failure.

Their moods lifted when they boarded the bus along with other members of the Lakeridge Cycling Club. Everyone was excited about seeing the races. Three hours later, they were seated in the stands at the Westwood Velodrome, eagerly waiting for the Olympic trials to begin.

The Velodrome was a cavernous building. Below the bleachers was a special oval track. Its sides were steeply banked so that it looked like a long, shallow bowl. It was marked off with lanes and different start and finish lines for races of various lengths. Cyclists in all sorts of uniforms were warming up, talking to their coaches, and checking their equipment. The air was thick with anticipation.

Doug consulted his program for the order of events. There was to be a series of sprints first, then a series of time trials. Last, they would see the individual pursuit races.

Doug thought back to the book he had read on track racing. Sprints, he knew, were 1,000-meter-long races, or three times around the track. But the cyclists were timed only for the last 200 meters. For the rest of the race, they were supposed to try to get in the best position for the final push. "Tactical maneuvering" was what Doug's book had called it. He wasn't really sure what that meant.

He looked up when the announcer called for the first race. Two cyclists lined up at the start. The flag went down and the race was on.

To Doug's surprise, the riders didn't seem to be pedaling hard. Instead, they looked to be concentrating on swerving back and forth, trying to outguess each other. Then, in the middle of the second lap, they came to a complete stop.

Billy almost fell off his chair.

"What happened?" he asked excitedly.

"Quiet down," Red said softly. "They're trying to psych each other out. It's part of the strategy. Whoever pulls out in front creates a slipstream that the other guy can draft on. Nobody wants to be the one doing the work only to have the other guy benefit from it."

Finally, just when Doug thought he couldn't stand the suspense any longer, one of the bikers bolted ahead and the race continued. During the final lap, their legs were a blur. Doug sat on the edge of his seat and yelled with the rest of the crowd. The noise was deafening, but it didn't faze the bikers. They powered across the finish line almost neck and neck.

Doug slid back into his seat. It was one of the most exciting races he'd ever seen. He couldn't wait for the next one to start.

For the next hour, he, Red, and Billy watched the sprinters. To add to the fun, Doug and Billy chose a biker to root for during each race.

"Red Shirt is going to out-psych his opponent," Billy whispered. "He looks determined."

"Nah," Doug whispered back. "Purple Shorts will blow him out of the water in the last lap!"

Sometimes Billy's man won and sometimes Doug chose the victor. Red just shook his head and grinned.

When the sprints were over, Red asked the boys if they were hungry. They were.

"Then let's head to the concession stand. Oh, and I

have a treat to give you afterward, too," he added mysteriously.

They wove their way through the spectators and found the snack bar. After some turkey sandwiches and a banana apiece, Red disappeared with a brief, "I'll be back."

A moment later he reappeared. "Well, here's the treat I promised!" Red called to them.

Doug saw that Red was no longer alone. A cyclist dressed in tight black shorts and an electric-blue top was standing with him. Doug recognized him as one of the sprinters they had watched earlier.

"This is Eric Sanders, an old cycling buddy of mine. Eric, this is Doug Cannon and Billy Torrant."

They all shook hands. "Red thought you guys might like to take a closer look at an indoor racing bike," Eric said. "Would you?"

Doug's eyes widened. "Would we ever!" he said excitedly. Billy nodded eagerly.

"Well, follow me to the locker room, then," Eric said. He led the way.

Eric's bike was different from anything Doug had ever seen. The wheels had no spokes. Instead, colorful disks filled the space between the tires and the

142

axles. The front tire was just a bit smaller than the back one. And instead of the curved handlebars of a ten-speed or the straight-across ones of a mountain bike, Eric's jutted out in front of his bike, curving just slightly upward at the end. Doug noticed something else, too.

"Where are the brakes?" he asked.

Eric laughed. "There are no brakes," he replied. "Not really. If you want to stop or slow down, you have to pedal backward."

Doug recalled that Red had told him about that at the beginning of the summer, when he was showing him his different bikes.

"Hey, and you have to keep pedaling all the time, right? Because there's no freewheel or gears!"

Eric nodded. "Right. And get a load of this." He slipped his index finger under the top tube of the bike's frame and lifted the bike easily. "It weighs less than fifteen pounds!"

"It's a beauty, Eric," Red said quietly.

Doug looked at him quickly. He realized for the first time that Red and Eric must have met when Red was still cycling competitively. He wondered how Red felt now that he was just a spectator.

Then a bell rang, signaling the start of a new series of races. They all thanked Eric and hustled out of the locker room.

But Doug couldn't stop thinking about Red. What would it be like to have a dream snatched out of your hands? Was it worth even trying for a distant goal if something like that could happen?

Red seemed to read his thoughts. "You know, I think Eric was more upset than I was that I had to give up racing after my accident. He said I was the best competition he'd ever had. He's a good friend. I never would have met him if it hadn't been for cycling. Kind of the way you two guys might not have met. Guess that's why I won't ever regret having taken up the sport, even though I lost out on my chance to go the distance."

Doug and Billy exchanged a glance. Doug could see that Billy hadn't looked at it that way, either. He realized, too, that he couldn't imagine what his life would be like without cycling. Even if he never reached beyond amateur races, like the Tour de Lakeridge, he knew he would continue with his chosen sport.

But he wasn't about to stop trying to reach beyond.

He turned his attention back to the action on the track. Yet even as he watched, cheered, and absorbed information about the various races, he felt sure that *his* destiny lay in a different arena — an outside arena composed of winding, tree-lined roads, not indoor oval tracks.

12

The next day, Billy couldn't stop talking about the races they'd seen.

"I think I'm a sprinter," he said."I love it when I can really put on the steam and zoom away. I like the idea of out-psyching my opponent on the track. These long runs are good training, but give me a burst of speed any day."

"Not me," Doug said. "I like to work at keeping a steady pace, just building it up slowly, then really going for it at the end. I think I'm a distance guy."

Billy looked at him curiously. "You said that so seriously," he remarked. "Like maybe it's not just for fun anymore."

Doug shrugged. "You know, I don't think it is. For me, anyway. And you, too, I think. I mean, where's the rest of our beginner's group? A bunch of quitters. They didn't have what it takes. We do!"

"All I know is I'd give anything to test out a real indoor racing bike like Eric Sanders had."

"Maybe you will someday. Listen, I say we make a pact — to stick together and help each other every step of the way. What do you say?"

Billy had stuck out his hand for Doug to shake. "Boy, you sure get all fired up!"

"I guess spending all that time with Red sank in. But hey, I'm still the fun-loving guy I always was!" He grabbed his water bottle, flicked it open, and squeezed it in Billy's direction. In return, he got a cold spray of water from Billy's bottle right in the face.

A bottle of champagne was popped open right behind Doug. He could almost feel a fizzy spray on the back of his neck.

As he moved away, a waiter with a tray of little sandwiches came up to him. He just shook his head. He'd stick to the raw veggies and fruit platter. He'd changed his biking gear for a tuxedo for the day and he was proud of the way he looked, all decked out in his fancy threads. If hanging on to that feeling meant passing on treats, well, he was ready to do just that.

After all, it was a treat just being here. Kate's wedding meant a day off from training. It was a good break, though, between the end of summer and the start of school. He'd begin on a whole new training schedule once classes started. Even though Billy would be going to a different school across town, they'd agreed to keep up their mutual effort.

"Looking good there, pal," said Red, munching on one of the little sandwiches.

Doug hadn't seen much of Red since the Westwood trip. Red was too busy getting ready for medical school.

"Are you through packing?" Doug asked.

"I still have a lot to do," Red admitted. "Your folks have been great, though. They said I could store any stuff in the carriage house I couldn't take with me." He took another bite of his sandwich. "It's going to be hard parting with my bikes, but I can't see having all three with me at school."

Doug's ears pricked up at that. "You're leaving your bikes behind?" he asked incredulously.

148

"Not all of them, just the racing bike. I haven't used it all summer, and I'm sure I won't have time for it this year. Seems a shame for it to be sitting around collecting dust, though. Maybe I'll try to sell it to someone who can use it."

"No!" Doug cried. Red looked at him with surprise. "I mean, not unless you really want to do that. You don't, do you?"

Red shook his head.

"Would you consider lending it to someone to try out? Because I know a guy who would give his right arm for a chance to try your bike."

Red looked puzzled for a moment. Then his face cleared and he started to grin. "I thought I'd read you wrong for a minute. But you're not talking about yourself, are you?"

Doug shook his head.

"Didn't think so. I had you pegged for a distance rider right from the start." He polished off the rest of his sandwich, then wiped his fingers on his napkin. "You tell Billy to stop by tomorrow. If the bike fits him, we'll see if we can't work something out."

Doug was about to cheer out loud when a tap on the arm stopped him.

149

"You're looking awfully happy. Want to dance?" Kate stood before him, looking like a princess but grinning wickedly.

Doug was taken by surprise. "I . . . I'm not sure I remember how," he answered lamely.

Kate laughed, caught his hand, and dragged him to the dance floor.

"Come on," she said. "It's just like riding a bicycle — it'll come right back to you!"

The grin on Red's face told Doug that he was making a fool of himself. But he didn't care. A tuxedo wasn't the most comfortable thing in the world to wear, but today he felt like a movie star in it.

13

Before Red left for medical school, he decided to let Billy work out with his racing bike. Jack Millman of the Lakeridge Cycling Club had taken an interest and agreed to oversee Billy's indoor training. Billy was on top of the world.

Doug was feeling the same way. Red, Kate, and Terry had all left for school the day before and he missed them all. But he found that the past summer had given him a confidence in himself he hadn't had the year before. He walked into this first day of classes with new energy.

Once his classmates got used to the "new" Doug Cannon, several of them seemed genuinely interested in biking. More than one expressed their disappointment that the Rails to Trails project had been abandoned.

Hearing them talk about it gave him an idea. He mentioned it to Billy during one of their daily rides.

"Hey, Billy, did you know that the old railbed passes behind both our schools?"

Billy shrugged. "So?"

"So what would you think about asking our schools to sponsor a joint road race to raise money for the Rails to Trails project? I bet parents would like to know their kids can bike to school without being on the roads."

Billy agreed that it sounded like a good plan. The first person they talked to about it thought so, too.

"We've been pretty disappointed that the project wasn't completed this summer," Jack Millman said. The boys had stopped by the clubhouse after their ride. "But we just couldn't think of a way to get people outside the club interested in it. Your idea could be the ticket!"

Jack said he would talk to Jimmy Bannister, the head of the project. If Jimmy was keen, then they would be in business. He promised to call them once he knew.

Later that night, the Cannons' phone rang. Doug jumped up to answer it.

"Doug, Jimmy loves the idea!" Jack's voice boomed. "He asked me to let you know that he's going to write a letter to your principals and the school board, telling them that you boys have his support one hundred percent. I'm going to do the same. Hopefully, you'll get the go-ahead soon. Then we can figure out how to organize this event. Can you and Billy stop by the clubhouse tomorrow to talk about it?"

Doug said he could and hung up. His head was spinning. For a moment, he wondered if he had bitten off more than he could chew.

To his relief, his parents offered to help in any way they could. "I'll bet my company would have some T-shirts made up for all participants," his father said.

"And I'm sure the PTA could get volunteers to help run it," his mother added.

Even Red Roberts called to encourage him. "I know you've got what it takes to make it happen," he said. Doug glowed at the praise. He hoped Red was right.

The next few weeks were filled with furious activity. Doug and Billy met with Jimmy and Jack, and they all agreed that the race would be open to students from the schools first, then to others in the community if there was room. The four of them created and distributed posters, flyers, and pledge sheets. They called all the remaining volunteers from the Rails project to get them involved. They mapped out a fifteen-mile route that ended with a short ride on the completed section of the path.

"The best way to convince people how important a bike path is is to let them compare a ride on one with a ride on a regular road! They'll never want to go back to the road after they try it," Jimmy said with a chuckle.

Doug and Billy each made speeches to their student councils. They were met with great enthusiasm and promises to help on the day of the event. They set the race for Columbus Day.

Two weeks before the event, Mr. Cannon came home with a surprise. He walked through the door carrying two big boxes.

"Open 'em!" he said to Doug.

Doug pulled back the cardboard top and saw a huge stack of blue-and-white T-shirts, his school's colors. The shirts in the other box were white-and-orange, the colors of Billy's school. The names of the schools were printed on the back. A picture of a biker decorated the front, with the slogan *"Get Rolling!"* above it.

Doug hugged his father hard. "These are great!" he cried. "Thanks, Dad."

His father beamed, then handed him a sheaf of papers. "Here are some more pledge sheets to add to your stack. They were sitting in the mailbox."

Doug's eyes widened when he counted them. "Wow! This makes over a hundred students participating in all! Good thing we decided to have staggered starts. It'd be a mob scene otherwise!"

"It's a good thing you held off opening it to the general public, too. I know you're both working toward a common goal, but I think the race itself will be more fun with just your rival schools competing against each other. And with these, you'll be able to tell who's riding for which school," his mother said, holding up one of each T-shirt.

14

Before he knew it, Columbus Day Weekend arrived. Saturday and Sunday were busy with last-minute activity. But by late Sunday afternoon, everything was done.

Jimmy Bannister had made sure the necessary roads were blocked off and the bike route clearly marked. Doug and Billy hadn't helped lay out the course because that would have given them an unfair advantage over the other bikers. But they had helped him set up the check-in booths. Mrs. Cannon and members of the PTA were organizing an after-race picnic on the football field.

Jack Millman had spent an hour with volunteers from the schools, teaching them how to mark down the cyclists' times and where to go for help in case of an accident. He himself would be overseeing the start of the race.

Both men took Doug and Billy aside at the end of the day on Sunday.

"We want to thank you boys personally for getting this thing rolling," Jimmy said. "And to know that if all the money pledged is collected, we'll have more than enough to finish the job in time for a grand opening next Memorial Day."

"I'm sorry it couldn't be sooner," Doug said.

"Hey, the fact that it's going to happen at all makes me happy!" Jimmy replied. "Let's just hope the good weather holds."

It did. Monday morning dawned bright and clear. There was a gentle breeze, but the sun made it warm enough to race in T-shirts.

Doug woke up a bundle of nerves. Up until now, he had been the race's organizer. Today, he was a competitor.

He arrived at the race check-in point at eight o'clock. He was in the first group of bikers, scheduled to start at ten. The second group would start half an hour later and a third at eleven. He wove his way through the crowd, registered his name, and got his T-shirt. Then he looked around for Billy. When he caught sight of him, he started to wave.

Then he stopped. He remembered how uptight Billy had been during the Tour de Lakeridge. Would he be that way again today? Doug just didn't know. Sure, they had raced each other for fun throughout the summer, but this was different.

Doug returned to his bike. He checked his water bottle and the air pressure in his tires. Out of the corner of his eye, he saw Billy start toward him, then stop and look at the white-and-orange T-shirt in his hand. He flung the shirt across his shoulder and disappeared into the crowd.

Billy senses it, too, Doug thought. We're friends, but today we're rivals. School rivals and individual rivals. Every man for himself.

Doug did his warm-up stretches, slipped his school T-shirt over his head, and waited for his start time to be called. He chatted with different people as they stopped by, but mostly he thought about the race ahead.

When the whistle blew and the announcement

called for the ten o'clock starters to gather, he was ready.

He couldn't help noticing that Billy was in the ten o'clock start, too.

All the contestants were in place. Doug recognized most of the cyclists wearing his school's colors — including a familiar face he hadn't expected to see: Pepper Meade. But there was no time to think about Pepper now. The huge time clock read 9:58.

Doug took a deep breath, adjusted his bike helmet slightly, and slipped a foot into his toe clip. He felt like a tightly coiled spring, ready to shoot forward as soon as Jack dropped the starter flag.

9:59.

The excited voices dwindled to a murmur, then fell silent altogether.

The clock blinked to 10:00. The flag in Jack's hand was a blur of color as it fell.

Doug took off, pedaling hard. Adrenaline pumped through his system, urging him to go faster and faster.

No! his head screamed. Don't overdo it too soon!

He concentrated on keeping a steady pace. Hunched tightly over the handlebars, he kept one careful eye on the road, the other on the cyclists around him.

That's when he saw Pepper Meade shoot out in front of the pack. He was pumping hard. Doug knew Pepper was trying to stay in the lead. He also knew that Pepper didn't realize how tiring that could be — or how a more knowledgeable biker could take advantage of him.

With a slight grin, Doug moved in behind Pepper. While the boy in front labored along, Doug eased up and drafted on the slipstream Pepper created.

As if sensing someone behind him, Pepper glanced over his shoulder. Doug saw a look of surprise register in his eyes before he turned back and redoubled his efforts.

He thinks I'm going to overtake him! Doug thought. Bet he never imagined he'd have to worry about *that!*

The idea gave him great satisfaction. He continued to ride right behind Pepper until the first checkpoint. Judging from the hangdog look on Pepper's face, he knew he'd have to find a different lead person for the second leg. Pepper was pooped.

The second leg of the route followed a series of hills

and sharp curves. Doug decided he'd be better off setting his own pace than following close behind an inexperienced biker over such difficult terrain.

At the first hill, he clicked through his gears without a thought. He passed three cyclists smoothly. A fourth was more difficult to maneuver around because he was weaving back and forth up the hill. Before he'd learned to use the gears effectively, Doug used to do the same thing. Now, looking at the fourth biker's labored movements, he wondered why he had ever thought such a tactic was efficient.

Doug crested the hill moments later.

"Thank God!" he heard another biker cry out. Then "Yeee-haaa!" and the same biker shot past him, pedaling fast — and moving at a dangerous speed.

Be careful! Doug wanted to scream. But he knew the biker was going too fast to hear him. Or to see what was on the road in front of him. Doug watched with horror as a squirrel darted right into the cyclist's path. He swerved to miss it but couldn't straighten out fast enough. His momentum carried him off the path and his bike collapsed beneath him. The squirrel scampered unharmed to the other side of the road.

Doug slowed.

"I'm okay, I'm okay," the biker said weakly. "Keep going, don't stop!"

Doug hesitated and glanced over his shoulder. One, two, three cyclists appeared at the top of the hill. Were they in any danger of hitting the fallen cyclist?

He turned back in time to see the rider limping out of harm's way, pulling his bike with him. Again, he yelled for Doug to continue. This time, Doug listened.

"I'll send a volunteer back for you!" Doug called as he took off. The biker waved.

For the rest of the second leg, Doug concentrated on the road in front of him. He pedaled hard into the curves and allowed his forward motion to carry him through. Other bikers passed him and he drafted off them when he could. Billy was one of them, but Doug didn't feel odd using him like this. He knew Billy would do the same in his place.

When he pedaled into the checkpoint, the first thing he did was alert a volunteer to the accident. Then he glanced at the time clock. He was fifteen seconds behind where he thought he should be.

While other bikers merely rolled into the checkpoint, called out their names, then hurried out again,

Doug slipped his water bottle from its clasp and took a long drink. He knew how important it was not to get dehydrated; the body needed fluids to keep performing at top notch. Only after he had drunk his fill did he call out his name and set out to complete the third and final leg of the race.

With fifteen seconds to make up, he pushed himself a little harder than he had before. The effort soon placed him in the lead.

The course curved gently to the right then moved from the regular road to the smooth, even bike path.

An eager spectator waved to him from behind a protective barrier. "Only two miles left to go!" the girl called out.

"Thanks!" Doug called back. To his shock, he heard another voice echo him. He turned his head slightly and saw a tall figure in a white-and-orange T-shirt move into place behind him. It was Billy. Doug suddenly realized no other bikers were in sight.

Doug knew that if he allowed Billy to continue drafting off him for the rest of the two miles, Billy would be much fresher for the final sprint to the finish line. Was Doug's time good enough to let that happen?

And even if it is, a little voice inside him said, do you really want to cross the finish line after him?

In answer, Doug veered sharply to one side, slowed, then veered back — behind Billy. It all happened so quickly that Billy didn't have time to react until it was too late. And then, Doug was watching him so closely that Billy's attempts at a similar maneuver were ineffectual. Doug had outsmarted his friend fair and square.

But suddenly, Billy took off.

It took Doug a moment to register why. Then he heard the shouts and cheers and realized that the finish line was closer than he thought. Billy must have figured it out, too.

Gritting his teeth, he downshifted and started to pedal for all he was worth. But Billy's crouched figure was still in front of him. By positioning himself directly in the middle of the path, he was making it difficult for Doug to pull around him.

Doug had to admit that Billy's tactic was smart. But the race wasn't over yet.

Pumping harder, he kept a steady eye on the path in front of him, waiting for his chance. The cheers from the crowd were growing louder. A few stragglers were running along the barrier beside them, yelling encouragement.

Then Billy made a mistake. He hugged the inside of a gentle curve too tightly, giving Doug room on the outside. Muscles straining, Doug drew up even with Billy just as the curve straightened.

They were now neck and neck. Even over the roar of the fans, Doug could hear Billy's steady breathing. The pavement below blurred past. Five hundred yards left. Then four hundred.

With his last bit of energy, Doug urged his legs to move a fraction faster. He couldn't be positive, but he thought that the front wheel of Billy's bike was slightly behind his now.

Three hundred yards.

Doug's T-shirt was soaked with sweat. He could feel the perspiration dripping down from under his helmet. Even his mitts were damp.

Two hundred yards. One hundred.

Doug raised his head and concentrated on the finish line. As he did, he heard a cry that seemed to come from a distant dream.

"Can-non! Can-non! Can-non!"

The sound of it thrilled Doug to his marrow. Then,

before he knew it, he was across the finish line and surrounded by congratulating fans.

A hand clapped him on the shoulder. "Way to go," a familiar voice said.

Doug turned to see Red Roberts grinning at him for ear to ear. Doug grinned back. No further words were needed right now. The winning time on the race clock spoke volumes. He knew his teacher had always believed in him, but he was glad Red had been there to see him triumph all the same.

Doug was attacked from behind in a big bear hug. "That was incredible! I can hardly believe it was you!" Kate cried. Terry was with her and added his hearty congratulations to hers.

Doug finally made his way through the crowd. He looked around for Billy but didn't see him anywhere. Disappointed and a little bit concerned about his friend, he wheeled his bike to the rack and locked it tight.

"Guess all that indoor practice has sapped my endurance a bit," a voice behind him drawled. Doug spun around and saw Billy smiling at him.

"Aw, I just got lucky at the end, on that curve," Doug said. "You had it all the way until then."

"Hey, I'm not looking for your sympathy," Billy replied, punching Doug playfully in the shoulder. "Now c'mon, stinky man, let's go grab a shower in the locker room before the picnic!"

An hour later, the football field was swarming with cyclists, their parents and teachers, and other members of the community. Like Doug and Billy, most of the contestants had showered but pulled their sweaty T-shirts back on over their clean clothes. Everyone wanted to show their school spirit and to stand out as participants in the race.

Doug and Billy grabbed a plate of sandwiches and some sodas, then found a place to sit in the bleachers. Doug saw his and Billy's parents laughing together a few rows down. Red was chatting with Jack Millman and Jimmy Bannister. All three men looked happy. Doug hoped it was because they had tallied up the pledges and found that they'd collected enough money to complete the bike path.

He didn't have to wait long to find out. Jimmy motioned for Doug and Billy to join him. So the boys stuffed the rest of their sandwiches in their mouths and tramped down the bleachers.

Jimmy produced a microphone that squealed when he turned it on.

"Well, at least I got everyone's attention," he said with a laugh. "I'd like to thank you all for being here today and for your generosity. Because of your donations and the combined efforts of the cyclists from both schools, we raised more than enough money to get that path finished once and for all!"

He held up his hand to quiet the cheers that followed.

"We'll do what we can before the snow flies, so anyone who wants to lend a hand, please see me over there" — he indicated a booth under one of the goalposts — "after the picnic. But first, here's a word from the fellows who made this whole thing possible."

Jimmy tried to hand the microphone to Billy. But Billy hurriedly pushed it into Doug's hands, then took a step back. Doug's mouth turned dry, but he faced his expectant audience squarely.

"Uh, I just want to say thanks, too," he mumbled. Out of the corner of his eye, he saw Red Roberts cross his arms over his chest and grin. And suddenly the words just started flowing out of his mouth. "But it

169

really wasn't me who made this happen. In fact, five months ago I would have laughed if you had told me I'd be standing here right now. Back then, I wasn't too interested in cycling — or anything besides videos and what was for dinner." The audience laughed warmly. "But thanks to someone, and he knows who he is, I got off my duff and found a whole new person inside of me!"

"So *that's* why you were so huge! You were two people the whole time!" Pepper Meade's unkind words rang out. Doug wasn't bothered by them. Pepper would always be Pepper until he decided to change. And until then, Doug decided he just wasn't worth worrying about.

"All I know is, you're looking at someone who's ready to follow a dream now. So here's to making dreams come true!"

The cheers echoed loud and long as Doug handed the microphone back to Jimmy.

Billy clapped him on the shoulder and said quietly, "That dream you were talking about, it wasn't just the bike path, was it?"

Doug shook his head. "You know it wasn't. In fact,

I think you know *exactly* what I was talking about, don't you?"

In reply, Billy stuck out his hand. Doug shook it solemnly.

By now, Red was bearing down on them. Doug looked up at his teacher, coach, and friend and said, "Who says everyone can't have an Olympic dream?"

How many of these Matt Christopher sports classics have you read?

- ❑ Baseball Flyhawk
- ❑ Baseball Pals
- ❑ The Basket Counts
- ❑ Catch That Pass!
- ❑ Catcher with a Glass Arm
- ❑ Challenge at Second Base
- ❑ The Comeback Challenge
- ❑ The Counterfeit Tackle
- ❑ The Diamond Champs
- ❑ Dirt Bike Racer
- ❑ Dirt Bike Runaway
- ❑ Face-Off
- ❑ Football Fugitive
- ❑ The Fox Steals Home
- ❑ The Great
  Quarterback Switch
- ❑ Hard Drive to Short
- ❑ The Hockey Machine
- ❑ Ice Magic
- ❑ Johnny Long Legs
- ❑ The Kid Who Only
  Hit Homers
- ❑ Little Lefty
- ❑ Long Shot for Paul
- ❑ Long Stretch at First Base
- ❑ Look Who's Playing
  First Base .

- ❑ Miracle at the Plate
- ❑ No Arm in Left Field
- ❑ Olympic Dream
- ❑ Pressure Play
- ❑ Red-Hot Hightops
- ❑ Return of the
  Home Run Kid
- ❑ Run, Billy, Run
- ❑ Shoot for the Hoop
- ❑ Shortstop from Tokyo
- ❑ Skateboard Tough
- ❑ Soccer Halfback
- ❑ The Submarine Pitch
- ❑ Supercharged Infield
- ❑ Tackle Without a Team
- ❑ Takedown
- ❑ Tight End
- ❑ Too Hot to Handle
- ❑ Top Wing
- ❑ Touchdown for Tommy
- ❑ Tough to Tackle
- ❑ Undercover Tailback
- ❑ Wingman on Ice
- ❑ The Winning Stroke
- ❑ The Year Mom Won
  the Pennant

All available in paperback from Little, Brown and Company